By the same author

TRAPS NEED FRESH BAIT

WIDOWS WEAR WEEDS

CUT THIN TO WIN

UP FOR GRABS

FISH OR CUT BAIT

TRY ANYTHING ONCE

SHILLS CAN'T CASH CHIPS

BACHELORS GET LONELY

KEPT WOMEN CAN'T QUIT

THE COUNT OF NINE

SOME SLIPS DON'T SHOW

YOU CAN DIE LAUGHING

BEWARE THE CURVES

TOP OF THE HEAP

ALL GRASS ISN'T GREEN

A. A. FAIR

(Erle Stanley Gardner)

WILLIAM MORROW & COMPANY, INC.
New York, 1970

G 172 al

ALL
GRASS
ISN'T
GREEN

1

The squeaky swivel chair in which Bertha Cool shifted her hundred and sixty-five pounds of weight seemed to share its occupant's indignation.

"What do you mean, we can't do the job?" Bertha asked, the diamonds on her hands making glittering arcs of light as she banged her palms down on the desk.

The potential client, whose card gave his name simply as M. Calhoun, said, "I'll be perfectly frank . . . er, uh, Miss Cool—or is it Mrs. Cool?"

"It's Mrs.," snapped Bertha Cool. "I'm a widow."

"All right," Calhoun went on smoothly, "I need the services of a first-class, highly competent detective agency. I asked a friend who is usually rather knowledgeable in such matters and he said the firm of Cool and Lam would take care of me.

"I come up here. I find that the Cool part of the firm is a woman, and that Lam is . . ." Calhoun looked at me and hesitated.

"Go ahead," I said.

"Well, frankly," Calhoun blurted out, "I doubt if you could take care of yourself if the going got rough. You won't weigh over a hundred and forty pounds soaking wet. My idea of a detective is a big man, aggressive, competent—heavy-fisted if the occasion requires."

Bertha once more shifted her weight. Her chair creaked indignantly. "Brains," she said.

"How's that?" Calhoun asked, puzzled.

"Brains is what we sell you," Bertha Cool said. "I run the business end. Donald runs the outside end. The little bastard has brains and don't ever forget it."

"Oh, yes . . . ah . . . doubtless," Calhoun said.

"Perhaps," I told him, "you've been reading too many mystery stories."

He had the grace to smile at that.

I said, "You've had a chance to look us over. If we don't look good to you, that door works both ways."

"Now, just a minute," Bertha Cool interposed, her diamond-hard eyes appraising our skeptical client. "You're looking for a detective agency. We can give you results. That's our forte. What the hell do you want?"

"Well, I *want* results," Calhoun admitted. "That's what I'm looking for."

"Do you know what the average private detective is?" Bertha Cool rasped. "A cop who's been retired or kicked out, a great big, beefy, bullnecked human snowplow with big fists, big feet and a musclebound brain.

"People like to read stories about private detectives who shove teeth down people's throats and solve murders. You tie up with an agency that is run by people who are all beef and no brains and you'll just ante up fifty dollars a day for every operative they put on the case—and they'll manage to load it up with two or three operatives if they think you can pay the tab. They'll keep charging you fifty bucks a day per operative until your money runs out. You *may* get results. You may not.

"With this agency we have one operative—that's Donald. I told you before and I'll tell you again, he's a brainy little bastard. He'll charge you fifty dollars a day plus expenses and he'll get results."

"You can afford to pay fifty dollars a day?" I asked, trying to get the guy on the defensive.

"Of course I can," he snorted. "Otherwise I wouldn't be here."

I caught Bertha's eye. "All right, you're here," I told him.

He hesitated a long while, apparently trying to reach a decision. Then he said, "Very well, this is a job that calls for brains more than brawn. Perhaps you can do it."

I said. "I don't like to work for a man who is a little doubtful right at the start. Why don't you get an agency which measures up more to your expectations?"

Bertha Cool glared at me.

Calhoun said thoughtfully, "I want to find a man."

"How old?" I asked.

"About thirty," he said. "Perhaps thirty-two."

"Give me a description."

"He's about five eleven, weighs a hundred and eighty-five or so. He has wavy hair, blue eyes, and has a magnetic personality."

"Picture?" I asked.

"No picture."

"Name?"

"Hale—H-a-l-e. The first name is Colburn. He signs his name C. E. Hale. I understand his close friends call him Cole."

"Last address?"

"Eight-seventeen Billinger Street. He had an apartment there, number forty-three. He left very suddenly. I don't think he took anything with him except a suitcase."

"Rent?"

"I believe it is paid up until the twentieth."

"Occupation?"

"I am given to understand he is a novelist."

"That location," I said, "is a bohemian neighborhood. There are lots of writers and artists living there."

"Exactly," Calhoun said.

"May I ask why you want to find Hale?"

"I want to talk with him."

"Just what do we do?"

"Locate the guy. Don't leave a back trail. Just give me the place where he is at present."

"That's all?"

"That's all."

"And Hale is a novelist?"

"I believe he is working on a novel. In fact, I know he is, but as to the nature of his writing I can tell you nothing. I know that he has a theory that when you talk about a story you either have a sympathetic or an unsympathetic audience.

"If the audience is unsympathetic it weakens your self-confidence. If the audience is sympathetic you are encouraged to talk too much and tell too much, which dissipates your creative energy in conversation rather than in writing."

"He is, then, secretive?"

"Reticent," he said.

I looked the guy over—casual slacks that were well pressed, a sports coat that had cost money, a short-sleeved Dacron shirt with a bolo tie. The stone in the bolo tie guide was a vivid green.

He saw me looking at it. "Chrysocolla," he said proudly.

"What's chrysocolla?" I asked.

"A semiprecious stone which ounce for ounce is probably worth more than gold. It is very rare. I might describe it as being a copper-stained agate. That doesn't exactly describe it, but it gives you an idea."

"Are you a rock hound?" I asked.

"So-so," he said.

"Find the stone yourself?"

"No, I traded for it. It's a beautiful specimen."

"When did you last see this Hale?" I asked.

Bertha said, "Now, just a minute, before we get down to brass tacks, we'd better finish with the preliminaries."

"Preliminaries?" Calhoun asked.

"Retainer," Bertha said.

He turned from me to study her.

"How much?"

"Three fifty."

"And what does that buy me?"

"Services of the agency, Donald doing the legwork at fifty bucks a day plus expenses. I furnish the executive management."

"At another fifty bucks a day?" he asked.

"It's all included in the one package," she said.

He regarded Bertha, sitting there as stiff as a roll of barbed wire, and somewhere around sixty-five, give or take a few years.

"Very well," he said.

"Got your checkbook handy?" Bertha asked.

He didn't like being pushed. He hesitated again, then reached in his pocket and brought out a billfold.

No one said anything while he hitched his chair over to the corner of Bertha Cool's desk and started counting out fifty-dollar bills.

Bertha leaned slightly forward, trying to see the interior of the billfold and make an estimate of the amount of money it held. He shifted his position so she couldn't see the interior.

There was silence while he counted out seven nice crisp fifty-dollar bills and put them on Bertha's desk.

"Now then," I said, "when did you last see Hale?"

"Is that important?"

"I think it is."

"I have never seen him."

"You've told me all you know about him?"

"No, I've told you all a good detective should need to know."

"And," I went on, "we'd like to know a little more about *you*."

He regarded me with uncordial eyes, then reached over to Bertha's desk and tapped the money with his fingers. "That money," he said, "gives you all of my background you're going to need."

He got to his feet.

"Where do we make reports?" I asked. "By mail or telephone? In other words, how do we reach you?"

"You don't reach me," he said. "I reach you. I have your phone number, you have my name. You know what I want."

"Just a minute," I said. "I want to take a look at a map of the city and get this location straight."

He hesitated halfway to the door.

I hurried down to my office and said to Elsie Brand, my secretary, "There's a man in slacks and sports coat just leaving Bertha's office, about thirty-one or thirty-two. I'd like to find out where he goes. If he takes a cab, get the number of the cab. If he has his own car, get the license."

"Oh, Donald," she said despairingly. "You know I'm a rotten detective."

"You're all right if you don't act self-conscious," I said. "Get out there in the corridor. Get in the same elevator he takes and try thinking about something else while you're riding down with him. If he acts suspicious, call off the job, but there's just a chance he'll be rather preoccupied and won't pay any attention to you."

I went back to Bertha's office just as Calhoun left the reception room. She was fingering the money. She looked up and said, "I don't like that smirking, supercilious son of a bitch."

I said, "He's putting on an act."

"What do you mean?"

I said, "He knew more about us than he wanted to let on. All that business about being surprised that you were a woman and that I wasn't built like a professional wrestler was part of an act."

"How do you know?"

"I sensed it."

"Why would he put on an act like that?"

"To get us on the defensive."

Bertha rang for her secretary and handed her the money. "Take this down and deposit it," she said.

I played a hunch. "This man that was just in," I said, "Calhoun. What did he say when he entered the office?"

"He wanted to know if Mrs. Cool was busy."

"Then he didn't just see the sign on the door, COOL & LAM, and know nothing about the firm."

She shook her head. "He knew about Mrs. Cool because he specifically asked for Mrs. Cool."

"Mrs. Cool?" I asked.

"Definitely, Mrs. Cool."

I glanced over at Bertha.

Her diamond-sharp eyes were blinking contemplatively.

I said, "The guy was very careful to keep from telling us anything about himself."

"As far as that is concerned, his money talked," Bertha said. "We don't give a damn who he is. We'll use up the three hundred and fifty and then we quit until he puts some more money in the kitty."

"I don't like it at all," I told her. "Let's take a look in the phone book."

"Oh, Donald, we can't look through all the different districts in the city. Here, let's take a look at this one district and see how many Calhouns there are."

"M. Calhouns," I reminded her.

Bertha opened the phone book, found the proper page and said, "Here are half a dozen of them right here. M. A. Calhoun, an M. M. Calhoun, a Morley Calhoun, an M. Calhoun and Company . . . the guy could be anybody."

Bertha had a reference book in back of her desk, *Prominent Citizens of California.* I pointed to it.

Bertha pulled the book down, opened it and said, "And here we've got a lot more Calhouns. Wait a minute, here's Milton Carling Calhoun who looks something like our man —Milton Carling Calhoun, the Second."

I looked at the picture. It could have been our client taken five years earlier. He was the son of Milton Carling Calhoun, the First. His father, who was dead, had been a stockbroker. Our man had graduated from college with honors, majored in journalism and had married Beatrice Millicent Spaulding.

There were no children. There was a list of clubs as long as your arm. Apparently the guy had never done anything in his life except inherit money.

"Fry me for an oyster," Bertha said, reading the copy. "The son of a bitch sure held out on us."

"Well, we've got him pegged now," I told her.

"Pegged is right," Bertha said.

I went down to my office and waited for Elsie Brand.

Elsie came back with the report. "He took a cab," she said, "a yellow cab. I managed to get the number. He evidently had the cab waiting at the curb because the flag was down and

16

as soon as the cabbie saw him coming he reached back and opened the door. Our man got in it and the cab drove away."

"You couldn't follow?"

"There was no cab I could grab in time," she said. "I told you, Donald, I'm a lousy detective."

"The number of the cab was what?"

"I got that all right. It was a Yellow Cab, number sixteen seventy-two."

"Okay, Elsie," I said. "You did a good job. I just wanted to make certain he was trying to give us a double cross. I'll take it from there and thanks a lot."

2

Eight-seventeen Billinger Street was an apartment house which had been converted from a three-story residence.

At one time that section of the city had been the site of imposing homes, but that had been many, many years ago.

The city had grown and engulfed the district. The luxurious homes had run downhill, then had been converted into rooming houses, or apartments with beauty parlors, small offices and nondescript stores on the ground floor.

I detoured a single-chair barbershop, found the stairs, climbed to the second floor, located Apartment 43 and stood for a moment at the door listening.

From Apartment 42, which adjoined it on the south, I could hear the steady clack of a typewriter, then an intermittent pause, then more clacking on the typewriter. From Apartment 43 there wasn't a sound.

I tapped gently on the door. There was no answer.

The typewriter in Apartment 42 was clacking away again. I stood there in the semi-dark hallway, undecided. I put my hand on the doorknob of Apartment 43. The latch clicked back. I pushed gently on the door for an inch or two. The door opened soundlessly.

I closed the door again and knocked, this time a little more firmly.

There was no answer.

I turned the knob, opened the door and looked inside.

It was a furnished apartment and someone had gone places in a hurry. There were a couple of empty cardboard cartons on the floor, and some old newspapers. Drawers had been pulled out, emptied, and left open. It was a one-room affair with a little kitchenette off to my right and an open door to a bath at the far end. There was a curtained closet; the curtain had been pulled back, exposing a wall bed. Empty wire clothes hangers were swinging dejectedly from a metal rod.

I wanted to go in and look around, but I had a feeling that it wasn't wise. I backed out and gently closed the door.

The typewriter in 42 had quit clacking. I heard steps coming to the door.

I raised my hand and knocked hard and loud on the door of 43.

The door of Apartment 42 opened. A woman in her late twenties, or perhaps early thirties, stood there looking at me appraisingly.

I smiled reassuringly at her and said, "I'm knocking on forty-three," and with that raised my hand and knocked again.

"Are you Colburn Hale's publisher?" she asked.

I turned to regard her searchingly. "Why do you ask?"

"Because Cole is expecting his publisher."

"I see," I said.

"You haven't answered my question," she observed.

"Should I?" I asked.

"I think so."

"Why don't you ask Mr. Hale when he comes back?" I said.

"Because I don't think he's coming back—perhaps I could help you?"

"Perhaps you could."

"Will you kindly tell me what's going on?" she asked.

I raised my eyebrows. "Is something going on?"

"You know it is. People came here in the middle of the night. They opened and closed drawers, put things in cardboard cartons, carried them downstairs."

"What time?"

"Around one o'clock in the morning."

"Did you see them?" I asked.

"I couldn't stand it any longer," she said. "I couldn't sleep with those people tramping back and forth, and I finally got up, put on a robe and opened the door, but they'd gone by that time."

"What time?"

"About one-thirty."

"How many people were there?"

"Two, I think."

"Colburn Hale and a friend?"

"I didn't have a chance to hear what was said. I didn't recognize Cole's voice. It might have been two other people for all I know. Now then, I'll ask you again, are you Cole's publisher?"

"No, I'm not," I said, "but I'm interested in talking to him before he talks to his publisher."

"Then you're a literary agent?" she asked.

"Well, not exactly, but—well, I can't tell you any more than that I'd like to talk to Hale before he talks to his publisher."

"Maybe you're making him an offer for a motion picture contract," she said.

20

I moved my shoulders in a deprecatory gesture and said, "That's your version."

She looked me over and said, "Would you like to come in for a minute?"

I looked dubiously at Hale's door. "I guess he's not home," I said. "You don't have any idea when he'll return?"

"I think he moved out. I don't think he's coming back."

"Behind in the rent?"

"I understand he pays his rent in advance from the twentieth to the twentieth. You don't get behind with your rent in this place. You either come up with the money or out you go."

"Hard-boiled like that, eh?" I asked.

"Very hard-boiled."

I followed her into her apartment. It was a little more pretentious than the apartment next door. Doors indicated a wall bed. There were a table, a battered typewriter desk, a portable typewriter and pages of a manuscript.

"You're a writer?" I asked.

She indicated a straight-backed chair. "Please sit down," she said. "Yes, I'm a writer, and if you're a publisher . . . well, I'd like to talk with you."

"Frankly," I told her, "I'm not a publisher. I don't even know whether I could help you or not. What kind of material do you write?"

"I'm writing a novel," she said, "and I think it's a *good* one."

"How far along are you with it?"

"I'm a little over halfway."

"Good characters?" I asked.

"They stand out."

"Character conflict?"

"Lots of it. I have suspense. I have people confronted with dilemmas which are going to require decisions, and the reader is going to be vitally interested in what those decisions are going to be."

"That's very interesting," I said. "How well do you know Colburn Hale?"

"Fairly well. He's been here only five or six weeks."

"What made you think I was his publisher?"

"I knew he was expecting a visit from his publisher and he had been working terribly hard on his novel, pounding away on the typewriter. He was a very good hunt-and-peck typist."

"Any idea what his novel was about?"

"No, we just decided we wouldn't tell each other our plots. And I have a basic rule. I never tell the details of a plot to anyone. I think it's bad luck."

I nodded sympathetically. "You and Hale were quite friendly?" I asked.

"Just neighbors," she said. "He had a girl friend."

"So?" I asked.

"Nanncie Beaver," she said. "I'm going to run over and see her sometime this afternoon and see what she knows. You see, we don't have telephones."

"A neighbor?" I asked.

"Up on eight-thirty," she said. "That's just a few doors up the street. She has Apartment Sixty-two B. I hope—I hope she knows."

"Is there any reason why she wouldn't?"

"You know how men are," she said suddenly.

"How are they?" I asked.

She flared up with sudden bitterness. "They like to play around and then if there are any—any responsibilities they duck out. They take a powder. They're gone. You can't find them."

"You think Colburn Hale was like that?"

"I think all men are like that."

"Including publishers?"

Her eyes softened somewhat and surveyed me from head to foot. "If you're a publisher," she said, "you're different. And somehow I think you are a publisher regardless of what you say."

"I'd like to be a publisher," I said.

"A subsidy publisher?"

I shook my head. "No, not that."

"You haven't told me your name."

"You haven't told me yours."

"I'm Marge Fulton," she said.

"I'm Donald Lam," I told her. "I'll be back again to see if Colburn Hale has come in. If he does come in, and you happen to hear him, will you tell him that Donald Lam is anxious to see him?"

"And what shall I tell him Donald Lam wants to see him about?"

I hesitated for several seconds, as though debating whether to tell her, then I said, "I think I'd better tell him firsthand. I don't want to be rude, but I think it would be better that way."

I got up and walked to the door. "Thanks a lot, Miss Fulton. You've been very helpful."

"Will I see you again?"

"Probably," I said.

"I think I'm writing a honey of a novel," she said.

"I'll bet you are," I told her.

She stood in the doorway watching me down the stairs.

I had a secondhand portable typewriter in my car. It fitted snugly into its case, and I got this portable out, climbed the stairs at 830 Billinger Street and found Apartment 62B was on the second floor. I tapped on the door and got no answer. I tentatively tried the knob. The door was locked. I stepped back a few paces and knocked on the door of Apartment 61B.

The woman who opened the door was a faded blonde with

traces of pouches under her eyes, but she was slim waisted and attractive. She was wearing a blouse and slacks, and I had evidently disappointed her because her facial expression showed that she had been expecting someone whom she wanted to see and I was a letdown.

I said, "You'll pardon me, ma'am, but I've got to raise some money in a hurry. I've got a typewriter here, a first-class portable that I'd like to sell."

She looked at me, then at the typewriter, and her eyes showed quick interest. "How much do you want for it?"

I said, "My name is Donald Lam. I'm a writer. I want money. I'd like to have you try out this typewriter and make me an offer. I'm desperately in need of cash. You can have this machine at a bargain."

She said, "I already have a typewriter."

"Not like this one," I told her. "This is in first-class shape, perfect alignment, and the work it turns out is—impressive."

I saw that interested her.

"Write a manuscript on this typewriter," I went on, "and it will stand out from the run-of-the-mill typing. Any editor will give it his respectful attention."

"How did you know I wrote?" she asked.

"I thought I heard the sound of a typewriter as I was walking down the corridor."

"Who referred you to me?"

"No one. I'm in a spot where I need cash, and I'm going to sell this typewriter to somebody before I leave the building."

"For cash?"

"For cash."

She shook her head and said, "Lots of people in this building use typewriters, but mighty few of them have the kind of cash that you would want."

I said, "Would it be too much to ask you to try out this

typewriter? I might make a trade, taking your machine, giving you this one and taking some cash to boot."

"How much to boot?"

"I'd have to see your machine first."

She looked at her wrist watch. "Come in," she said.

The apartment was a two-room affair with a partial division screening off the kitchenette. A portable typewriter sat on a rather battered card table with a folding chair in front of it. There were pages of manuscript on the card table and the apartment gave evidences of having been well lived in. It wasn't exactly sloppy, but it wasn't neat.

"You're living here alone?" I asked.

Her eyes suddenly became suspicious. "That's neither here nor there. Let's look at your portable," she said, picking her portable up off the card table and setting it on a chair.

I opened my portable and put it on the card table.

She put some paper in and tried it out. She had the hunt-and-peck system, but she was good at it.

"What do you write?" I asked. "Novels, articles, short stories?"

"Anything," she said. "I am Annaemae Clinton."

I looked around a bit. There were writers' magazines and a book containing a list of markets. There was a pile of envelopes on a shelf which I surmised contained rejected stories which had been returned from the editors.

She swiftly picked up the pages of manuscript that were on the card table, took them over to the chair which held the typewriter and put them face down on top of the typewriter.

"This is a pretty good machine," she said.

"It's in perfect condition."

"What kind of a trade?" she asked.

"I'd want to take a look at your machine."

She went over to the chair, picked up the manuscript pages

from on top of the typewriter, moved them over to a bookcase, brought the typewriter over, shoved my machine out of the way and put her typewriter down on the card table. Then she rather grudgingly handed me a sheet of paper.

The typewriter was an ancient affair which ran like a threshing machine and the type was pretty much out of line. In addition to which the type faces were dirty. The *e* and the *a* gave pretty poor impressions.

"Well?" she asked.

I said. "I'll take your typewriter, give you mine, and take forty dollars in cash."

She thought it over for a while, then said, "Let me try your machine again."

She did more typing this time. I could see she wanted it.

"Twenty-five dollars," she said.

"Forty," I told her. "This machine is like new."

"Thirty."

"Make it thirty-five and it's a deal."

"You're a hard man to do business with."

"I need the money, but I've got a good typewriter here. Your machine needs lots of work done on it."

"I know that."

She was silent for a while, then said, "Would you take fifteen dollars down and twenty dollars in two weeks?"

I shook my head. "I need money."

She sighed reluctantly. "I can't cut the mustard," she said.

"All right," I told her. "I'll try next door. Who's your neighbor in Apartment Sixty-two B?"

"There isn't any."

"Not rented?"

"It was, but she moved out, a woman by the name of Beaver, Nanncie Beaver. She spelled her first name N-a-n-n-c-i-e."

"A writer?"

"I guess so. She used to do a lot of clacking on the type-writer. I didn't ever see her by-line on anything."

"Sociable?"

"Not particularly—but a nice sort. She moved all at once. I didn't know anything about it until yesterday when she moved out."

"Boyfriends?"

"I wouldn't know. We live our own lives up here. There's a couple in Sixty B, name of Austin. I don't know what they do. I think he has a job somewhere. I don't know if she writes. I never hear a typewriter over there. I think she's some sort of an artist. They keep very much to themselves. When you come right down to it, that's the way people live in this section."

She thought for a moment and then added, "And it's the only way to live."

"Did Miss Beaver give you any hint she was moving out?" I asked.

"No, I didn't know anything about it until she started moving out cardboard boxes and suitcases."

"Transfer man?"

"Taxicab," she said. "She made some arrangements with the driver to help her."

"That's strange about the cardboard boxes and the suit-cases," I said.

"Well, she had cardboard cartons. There must have been a half a dozen of them that were sealed with tape and had stationary pasted on the side. She took those first and then in about thirty minutes came back and got the suitcases."

"Taxi driver helped her all the time?"

"Yes."

"A Yellow Cab?"

"Yes, at least I think so."

"Same taxi driver?"

"I wouldn't know. Heavens! *Why* are you so interested in Nanncie Beaver?"

"I'm darned if I know," I told her, "but I'm a great one to try and put two and two together and understand people. I regard everyone as a potential story. What you have told me just arouses my curiosity."

"Well, she's gone. You can't sell her a typewriter now."

"You don't think she'll be back?"

She shook her head. "Tell me, what's the best deal you'll make on a trade?"

I looked at her typewriter again. "I can't offer you very much encouragement. This is in bad shape. It needs cleaning, oiling, a general overhaul."

"I know. I keep putting things off, and when you're free-lancing on articles and things, you don't have much money. I can't get along without the machine—and I don't have much money—so I can't afford to put it in the shop. Some of my checks I get for stories are for less than five dollars . . . the cheaper magazines, you know."

"Tough luck," I said. "Perhaps if your manuscripts looked —well, more professional, you could make better deals."

"That's what I was thinking. That's why I wanted to see what kind of a trade you'd make—but I can't go without eats, and rent is due in two weeks."

"I can't better the proposition I've made you," I said.

"You don't feel you could take fifteen dollars down and then come back in two weeks and get twenty dollars. I've had a story accepted. I'll have the twenty for sure."

"I'm sorry," I said. "I couldn't do it. Who else is in the building that you know that might be interested in type-writers?"

"No one," she said. "There are only four apartments on this floor. The fourth apartment is rented by some kind of a business woman. She's up and off to work every morning. I don't know anything about the people on the upper floor."

I put my typewriter back in its case.

"I'm sorry," I said. "I'll try the building next door. Do you know anything about it?"

She shook her head. "We don't pay much attention to our neighbors," she said. "We have our friends and that's that. I sure would like to have that typewriter."

"I wish I could afford to sell it on the basis of the offer you've made, but I have my own living to think of."

"Do you write?"

"Once in a while."

"You look prosperous. You look as if you didn't have trouble selling."

"Can you tell that by looking at me?"

"Yes, there's an incisive something about you, an atmosphere of assurance. You take us free-lance writers that get beaten down with rejections and after a while there's a general aura of frustration and futility which clings to us. I've seen it happen to others and I think it's happening with me."

"Tell you what I'll do," I told her. "You've been a good sport. I'll take a chance. Give me fifteen dollars and your typewriter, and I'll come back in two weeks for the twenty."

"Will you do that?" she asked, her face lighting up.

I nodded.

"Oh, that's wonderful! I've been thinking about the appearance of my work lately. It does look sort of—well, amateurish."

"A fresh ribbon wouldn't hurt any on your typewriter," I said.

"Fresh ribbons cost money," she said, "and money doesn't grow on bushes."

She went into a closet, fumbled around for a while, then came out with two fives and five dollars in one-dollar bills.

I handed her my typewriter, put her typewriter in its case, and said, "Remember, I'll be back in two weeks. I hope the new machine brings you luck."

"It will. It will! I know it will!" she said. "I'm feeling better already. You said your name was Lam?"

"Donald Lam."

"I'll have the money for you, Donald. I just know I will. I'm assured of that sale. I feel it in my bones. I would have done a little bit better on this first installment, only I have to eat and I'm saving out enough for hamburger. You can't do good work when you're *really* hungry."

"That's right."

She saw me to the door, then on impulse put her arms around me and kissed me on the cheek. "I think you're very wonderful," she said.

I took her battered-up typewriter and went back to my car, thinking over the information I had obtained about Nanncie Beaver.

Two trips in a taxicab. Cardboard cartons, one trip, which lasted less than half an hour; and then suitcases on the *second* trip, and she didn't come back after the second trip.

I went back to the directory and found the card that was marked MANAGER.

I went to the manager's apartment. She was past middle age, heavy and cynical. "Do you have a vacancy?" I asked.

"I'm going to have one, Sixty-two B on the second floor. It's a nice apartment."

"Can I take a look at it?"

"Not right now. It isn't cleaned up yet. The tenant just moved out yesterday and left things in something of a mess."

"I'll make allowances for that."

"I can't go up with you now. I'm expecting a long-distance call."

"Let me have the key and I'll take a look," I said.

"What do you do?" she asked.

"I'm a writer."

She shook her head. "Writers are pretty poor payers. They mean all right, but they can't come up with the money when they don't have it, and there's lots of times when they don't have it."

"What do you want for the apartment?" I asked.

"Fifty-five dollars," she said.

I said, "I'm a little different from the average writer. I would be able to give you the first month's rent down and fifty-five dollars for the last month's rent. Anytime I didn't pay up you could take the rent out of that second fifty-five dollars."

"Well, now, that's something different," she said. "You must be a very successful writer."

"I'm getting by," I told her.

She handed me a key. "Remember, the apartment is in an awful mess. I'm going to have it cleaned later on today."

"Sure," I said. "I'll make allowances."

I went back up the stairs and into Apartment 62B.

It was in something of a mess. Papers were strewn around on the floor. Other papers had been hastily crumpled and thrown into the wastebasket. Some of the drawers were half open.

I smoothed out the crumpled papers. Most of them were the type of form letter that is sent out on direct mail advertising. One of the papers was typed and listed a series of articles, three books, with the title and the author, and then the list went on: half a package of first-page typewriter paper, a full package of copy paper, pencils, pens, erasers, typewriter ribbons, envelopes, writers' market data.

There was nothing to tell me why she'd pulled that piece of paper out of the typewriter, crumpled it up and thrown it in the wastebasket.

At the top was the name—NANNCIE ARMSTRONG, Box 5.

I took the paper, folded it up, left the apartment, gave the keys to the manager and said I was thinking it over and that I'd like to see the apartment after it was cleaned up.

I drove to my apartment, got the classified telephone book, and looked under STORAGE.

There was a storage company, the International, which had a branch within about five blocks of Billinger Street, where Nanncie Beaver had lived.

I went back out to the car and drove over to the Yellow Cab Company. The dispatching operator said, "I had a cab yesterday that picked up some cardboard cartons at eight-thirty Billinger Street and took them to the International Storage branch that is about five blocks away . . . Was there trouble?"

"Quite the contrary," I said. "I found that cab driver very alert, very competent, very courteous. I have some other things I want done and I'd like to get him."

"That cab might be rather hard to locate," the operator said.

"Your cabs report in on what they're doing," I said. "This cab reported in that it was on Billinger Street and was taking a bunch of cartons to the International Storage Company; then the cab picked me up with my suitcases."

Since I knew that the cab drivers reported by address and not by customer, I knew the dispatcher had no way of knowing whether the customer had been a man or a woman.

I pushed a five-dollar bill through the wicket. "It's quite important to me," I said. "If a box of chocolates would help refresh your recollection, this would give the needed stimulus."

"That won't be necessary," she said.

"It might help," I told her.

She almost absent-mindedly reached for the five-dollar bill. "It might take a little while to look this up," she said.

"I'll wait."

"I . . . wait a minute, I've got it right here. It was cab two twenty-seven A. These drivers work in shifts, you know. The cabs keep busy all the time, theoretically twenty-four hours a day. One cab driver returns the cab to the garage, the next driver picks it up."

"I know," I said, "but this driver was on duty in the morning and . . ."

"Then he'd probably be on duty at this hour," she said.

"Could you locate him," I asked, "and have him go back to Eight-thirty Billinger Street? I'll be waiting there for him."

"You want to get this particular cab?"

"This particular *driver*," I said.

"All right," she told me, making a note. "I'll notify him. You'll be waiting there?"

"I'll be waiting there at the foot of the stairs."

I drove my car back to 830 Billinger Street and waited twenty-five minutes before a Yellow Cab drove up.

The driver got out and looked around.

"You did a job for me yesterday," I said, "moving some cartons to the International Storage Company."

He looked at me thoughtfully. "It wasn't for you," he said. "It was . . ."

"I know," I told him. "It was for my assistant, Nanncie Beaver, who was moving out of Apartment Sixty-two B. Now then, there's been a mix-up on some of the stuff that she took with her and some of the cartons that were left at the storage company. I'm going to have to check and you can help me. First, we'll go to the International."

He took the ten dollars I handed him and said, "Is this on the up and up?"

"Of course it's on the up and up. I'm just trying to get some stuff straightened out. I think Nanncie made a mistake in packing up in the apartment and put a manuscript in which I'm interested in one of the boxes that was stored."

"Okay," he said, "let's go."

He pulled down the flag and I rode with him to the branch of the International Storage Company.

"Just wait here," I said. "I won't be long."

I walked in and told the girl at the desk, "My assistant brought in a bunch of cartons from our apartment at Eight-thirty Billinger Street yesterday. The cab driver out there made the delivery. She signed the papers. There's been a mix-up in the number of boxes. I want to find the bill of lading, or whatever it is you issue, and check on the number of boxes."

She took it as a matter of course. "What name?" she asked.

"Nanncie Armstrong," I said taking a shot in the dark.

She ran down an alphabetical list, said, "Here it is. There were six cardboard cartons."

"Only six?"

"Only six."

"Then six A is missing," I said. "I'll have to try to locate it. Thank you very much."

I could see that there was just a faint hint of suspicion in the girl's eyes, so I didn't press my luck. I went back to the taxicab and said, "There's been a mix-up somewhere. We'll go back to Eight-thirty Billinger Street."

On the road back, I said, "You took my assistant and her suitcases somewhere after she had stored the boxes?"

"That's right."

"Airport?" I asked.

He turned around with sudden suspicion. "Not the airport," he said.

I laughed and said, "She's always trying to save money. I suppose she went by bus. I told her to take the plane."

"I took her to the bus depot," he admitted.

I didn't ask any more questions but paid off the meter when he stopped at Billinger Street and started for the stairs. "I've got to find that extra box somewhere," I told him. "I suppose

34

Nanncie left it with the manager for me to pick up. We're giving up the apartment, you know."

"So I gathered," he said, then looked at the tip I had given him, nodded his head, said, "Okay," and then drove away.

I got in my car, drove to my apartment and picked up a cardboard carton, took some old newspapers and three or four books that I didn't care much about, sealed everything in the box and typewrote a sheet, NANNCIE ARM-STRONG, Box 6 A.

I made up a detailed fake inventory and taped the sheet of paper on the carton.

I then went back to the International Storage Company and came in lugging my dummy box with a cheerful smile on my face.

"All right," I said, "I chased down the box that was lost. This is box number six A. Put it with the others if you will, please."

She took the box.

I said, "I presume there may be a little more to pay on the storage."

"It won't amount to much. We get two months' storage in advance on jobs of this sort. There were six packages and she paid for them—there'll only be fifty cents due on a package this size, which we'll put in with the others."

"Fine," I told her, handed her fifty cents, and started for the door, then checked my step as though struck by an afterthought.

I walked back and said, "I'm sorry, but I'm going to have to have a receipt."

"But Miss Armstrong has the receipt," she said.

"I know, for six cartons. Now there are seven, counting this one which is numbered six A."

She frowned a minute, then said, "All right, I'll make out a separate receipt."

She took a piece of paper, scribbled "One cardboard carton added to Nanncie Armstrong's account, General Delivery, Calexico, California," marked "50¢ paid," signed the receipt with her initials and handed it to me.

"You can put this with the others and it'll be all right," she said.

I thanked her and walked out.

Nanncie Armstrong had taken a Greyhound Bus. She had given an address, General Delivery, in Calexico. She didn't have a car of her own. Colburn Hale hadn't left the faintest sign of a backtrack, but putting two and two together, it was a good bet that he and Nanncie Beaver were planning a meeting.

I drove back to my apartment, picked up a suitcase, threw it in the back of the agency heap and started for Calexico.

3

I drove through the Beaumont and Banning Pass with the San Gorgonio Mountains on my left and San Jacinto towering high on my right.

We made a charge to clients of fifteen cents a mile for the agency car, and as the miles clicked off I wondered how Bertha and the client were going to react to the expense account.

Bertha was always screaming to keep expenses down because that meant more of a fee for the agency, and driving down to Calexico was going to put a big nick in the client's three hundred and fifty bucks—by the time I charged mileage and my living expenses on top of that.

There was still snow on the north side of San Jacinto, which towers more than two miles above sea level, but it was hot down in the valley, and by the time I had left Indio behind and the road dropped down to below sea level it was too hot for comfort. Bertha would never listen to having an agency heap with air conditioning. She claimed all of our driving was around the city and air conditioning was more of a nuisance than a benefit there.

I hadn't reported to the office or told Bertha where I was going. I knew she'd have a fit. But the Calexico lead was the only one I had.

It was late afternoon when I reached Calexico.

Calexico and Mexicali are twin cities. Calexico on the north, Mexicali on the south, and the international boundary fence between the United States and Mexico is about all that separates the two cities.

Now, Nanncie had no car. She had taken a bus. She evidently wasn't too flush with money. I felt she wouldn't be staying at the rather swank De Anza Hotel. In fact, I wasn't sure that she was in Calexico at all. The only thing I had to go by was that address of General Delivery. She could very well have crossed the border and gone into Mexicali.

I knew that I was going to have to do a lot of routine work.

I had a decoy envelope with me which I had addressed to Nanncie Armstrong at General Delivery, and I dropped it into the mail.

Unless you're a Federal officer, the post office will give out no information about its customers, but the decoy envelope is a good way to get you the information you want in a reasonably small town.

The decoy envelope is manufactured especially for that purpose. It is too big to be put in a pocket or in a purse. It has red and green stripes on it so it is as conspicuous as a bright-red necktie at a funeral. You mail the envelope, get a parking place where you can watch the door of the post office and keep an eye on the people who come and go, particularly at about the time the mail is being distributed.

If the subject calls for mail at the General Delivery window and gets the decoy envelope, he can't put it in his pocket if he's a man, or if it is a woman it won't fit in her purse. The subject comes out the door holding the decoy envelope and usually pauses on the sidewalk to open it.

The decoy envelope has an ad in it, a routine solicitation to buy real estate, and the subject thinks it's just part of a broadside mailing campaign.

The detective covering the post office gets a good look at the subject and a chance to follow.

After I mailed my envelope I drove up and down the street, listing the motels and rooming houses. I didn't have too much hope here because I had a feeling the subject had crossed over to Mexico but would continue to get mail at Calexico.

However, having made out a list of the motels, I got to a public telephone and started making calls.

With each one I said, "This is the Acme Credit Agency. You have a woman who is registered with you who doesn't have an automobile but who came in a taxicab. Her name is Debora Smith. Can you tell me what unit she's occupying?"

I got a turndown in three places and then at the Maple Leaf I struck unexpected pay dirt.

"We have a woman such as you describe," the voice said, "who came here by taxicab carrying two suitcases, but her name is not Debora Smith."

"What unit does she occupy?" I asked.

"Unit twelve."

I said, "The party I want is about sixty-two years old. She comes from New York City. She's about five feet six, rather slender, and—"

"No, no, no," the voice interrupted me. "This person is around twenty-six with auburn hair. She's medium height, has a good figure and . . ."

"That's not the one I'm after," I said. "My party is in the sixties and rather slender, a little above average height."

"I'm sorry, we have no one by that description."

"Thank you very much," I said, and hung up.

I got in the agency car, drove to the Maple Leaf, registered and was assigned to Unit 7.

It was a fairly good motel with a small swimming pool, a patio and some beach chairs around the pool.

It was getting late, but a couple of kids and a matronly woman were in the pool.

I put on my suit, went to the pool, hesitated about getting in, and then went to one of the beach chairs and relaxed, sitting where I could keep my eye on Unit 12.

It was no dice.

It got dark. The swimmers left the pool and I was getting chilled. I went in and dressed, sat in my parked car and kept my eye on Unit 12.

Nothing happened until twenty minutes to nine when my party came in.

I had her spotted as soon as I saw her, even before she fitted the key to the door of Unit 12. She was a nice looker. She arrived by taxicab and she looked dejected.

I waited until I saw she was headed for Unit 12; then I started the agency heap, overtook the taxicab, which was headed toward the border, and signaled him over to the curb.

The driver was an alert-looking Mexican.

"Is this a Mexican cab?" I asked.

He nodded.

"I want to go across the border," I said, "but I don't want to take my car. Can I park it here and go across with you?"

"It is illegal for me to pick up a fare on a return trip," he said.

"I came across from Mexicali with you," I told him. "Don't you remember?"

White teeth flashed in the dim light from the instrument panel. "Now I remember," he said. "Get in."

I parked and locked my car and got in the cab.

"We have to make a little detour to cross the border," he said, "but we make a flat rate. Where do you want to go?"

He looked at the five dollars I handed him.

"You just delivered a young woman at the Maple Leaf Motel," I said. "Where did you pick her up?"

"Oh ho," he said, "a detective!"

I grinned at him and said, "A caballero who is lonesome. I would like very much to pick up that young woman, but I don't think the usual approach would be any good."

"She came to me," the driver said, "from the Monte Carlo Café in Mexicali."

"And that is where you are taking me," I said.

Again his teeth flashed in a wide smile. "But certainly," he said.

Pedestrians can walk straight across the border of Calexico, but the automotive traffic has to make a detour around through a side street, then along a street which parallels the border, until it comes to the north and south road where it is stopped by a traffic signal, then has to make a right-hand turn in order to cross into Mexico.

This gave me time for a little conversation with the driver.

"You Mexican taxicab drivers are permitted to drive across and deliver fares in the United States?"

"Sí, señor," he said. "And the American cab can cross into Mexico and deliver a fare in Mexicali, but we are not supposed to pick up a fare in Calexico to return to Mexico." He shrugged his shoulder. "Perhaps there is trouble. I do not know. If I am unfortunate I could have a fine."

I thought perhaps that was an approach for a touch so said nothing.

After a while he said, "That is peculiar, that case of the woman who goes to the Maple Leaf Motel."

"Yes?" I asked.

"Yes," he said.

There was a period of silence.

This time I interpreted the silence correctly and he had made the right approach. I produced another five-dollar bill.

He took it eagerly, said. "I have much trouble at home. I have four children, another is coming, and the cost of living is very high."

"The cost of living is very high for me," I said. "What is peculiar about the woman?"

"She does not speak Spanish," he said. "The waiter that she asked to call the cab called me. He told me he had a passenger for me to deliver in the United States. Then he told me she had gone to the café, she had ordered one drink. She had waited, waited, waited. Then she had ordered another drink. She had waited, waited, waited. Then she ordered a meal and she ate very, very slowly, very slowly, indeed, señor . . . She was waiting for someone who did not come. Does that help, señor?"

"It may help," I said.

Then he said, suddenly stopping the car, "Get out, please, and walk the one block until you have passed the border. I will be waiting for you there and I will deliver you the rest of the way. It is better this way. I cannot afford the trouble."

I got out of the cab at the corner, walked down the street and crossed the border. I would not have been surprised if I had never seen the cab driver again, but he was there waiting to drive me the four blocks to the Monte Carlo Café.

The café was a fairly large restaurant, although the entrance was modest, a single room with a bar at the back and a few tables. There was a door leading into another room and then a door into still another room. These rooms had many tables and there was a good sprinkling of customers.

There was quite a bit of family trade. The restaurant was quiet, conservative, respectable, and the aroma of the food was so appetizing that I sat down and ordered a meal.

While the meal was coming I found a telephone and put through a call to Bertha's unlisted number at her apartment.

"Fry me for an oyster!" Bertha gasped. "You can disappear longer and make fewer reports! Where the hell are you now?"

"Mexicali," I said.

"Mexicali!" she screamed at me. "What are you doing down there?"

"Following clues."

"You'll use up all of the retainer money in expenses," she complained.

"I've used up plenty of it so far."

"That's the worst of you. You throw money away as though it grew on bushes. Why don't you ever make a report?"

"I didn't have anything to report."

"Well, our client has been chewing his fingernails as far as the elbow."

"You've seen him again?"

"Have I seen him again! He's been in once, and he's been on the telephone three times. He hung up about half an hour ago and told me if you reported before midnight tonight to let him know. I was to give you his number and you were to call him at once."

I said, "I'm following a lead that has taken me south of the border. That's all I can tell him. You call him and tell him I'm on a hot trail—and, by the way, if he's so worked up about things it might be a good plan to touch him for another hundred and fifty."

"He's worked up all right," Bertha said, "but he doesn't seem to be in a generous mood. He's in an anxious mood. You'll have to call him yourself. The number is six-seven-six-two-three-o-two."

"All right. I'll call him. I'm staying in Calexico. I followed a lead across to Mexicali, and I expect to have something definite by tomorrow."

"You're on a hot trail?"

"A hot trail."

"At fifteen cents a mile," Bertha said.

"We're making money at fifteen cents a mile," I reminded her.

"Not when it cuts into our retainer," Bertha said. "It's easier to sell personal services at fifty dollars a day than cars at fifteen cents a mile."

"All right," I told her. "This case has been more complicated than we had anticipated and there'll be a bill for expenses."

"Where are you going to be tonight, Donald? Where are you staying?"

"In Unit Number Seven at the Maple Leaf Motel in Calexico. I think that the man we want is going to show up within twenty-four hours. I'll give you a ring just as soon as I get anything definite."

"Well, call up and tell our client," Bertha said. "He's wearing holes in the carpet."

"All right. I'll call him," I promised, "but I don't want him messing into the play."

"Be sure to call him right away," Bertha said. "He said if I heard from you before midnight you were to call him. You have the number—six-seven-six-two-three-o-two. Now, play it cool, Donald, and keep the guy happy with what we're doing."

I promised her I would and hung up.

I called the number Bertha had given me.

Calhoun's voice came rasping over the line. "Hello, who is it?"

"Donald Lam," I said.

"Well, it's about time!" he exclaimed.

"About time for what?"

"About time for you to make a report."

"You didn't hire me to make reports," I said. "You hired me to find somebody."

"Have you found him?"

"No."

"Where are you?"

"At the moment I'm in Mexico."

"In Mexico!"

"That's right."

"What the hell are you doing in Mexico?"

"Looking for the person I'm supposed to find."

"Well, you're not going to find him down there."

"Are you sure?"

When he hesitated at that one, I said, "I've followed what I think is a live lead."

"What is it?"

"His girl friend," I said.

"His what?"

"His girl friend."

"Who?"

"I don't like to mention names over the telephone, but she lives not too far from where the man you want lived and she disappeared at about the same . . ."

"Don't tell me you've found her?"

"I've found her."

"The hell you have!"

"Why?" I asked. "Is that important?"

"I agree with you, Lam," he said, his voice suddenly friendly. "That's a very, very live lead. Is she near where you are now?"

"Yes."

"Where?"

"I'm talking over a public telephone," I said, "on the south side of the international border. I don't want to go into details."

"Damn it, Lam," he said, his voice sharp with irritation, "*I'm* the one to take the responsibility. *I'm* the one who's paying you. Where is she?"

I said, "She's on the other side of the line at Calexico."

"Where?"

"At a motel."

"What's the name of the motel?"

I hesitated a moment, then said, "The Maple Leaf. She's in Unit Number Twelve, but I don't think our man is going to join her there. I think the rendezvous is going to be somewhere south of the border."

"Do you have any idea why?"

"Not at this time. I had quite a job locating her. She tried to cover her back trail and she's here under an assumed name."

"What name?" he asked.

I said firmly, "I'm not going to give that out over this telephone. What's your interest in the girl? You hired us to find somebody else."

"I'm interested in finding out what you're doing. When I spend money, I want to know what I get in return for it."

I said, "Hello, operator . . . operator . . . you've cut me off . . . operator."

Then I gently slid the receiver into its cradle and went back to enjoy my dinner.

It was a wonderful dinner. The sweet-meated lobsters of Baja California, a side dish of chile con carne, not the bean dish which is really a misnomer, but chunks of tender meat swimming in hot, red sauce.

There were also tortillas and *frijoles refritos*.

Just as I was finishing my meal a man came up to the manager at the cash register, which was directly behind the table where I was sitting.

"I was expecting to meet someone here," he said, "but I

46

was delayed on the road. Did anyone leave any messages for me?"

"What's the name?"

"Sutton."

The manager shook his head. "No messages, Señor Sutton."

The man looked around the restaurant dubiously.

The manager said, "There was a señorita, an American girl, who came here and waited and waited, then had dinner and departed in a taxicab."

"But no message?" Sutton asked.

"I am sorry, señor, no message."

The man walked out.

I grabbed a bill, threw it at the cashier, didn't wait for the check or any change, but hurried to the door. I was in too much of a hurry. My waiter grabbed me. "The check, señor. You have not paid."

"I paid," I told him. "I put money on the counter at the cash register."

"It is not possible to pay without the check," he insisted.

Trouble in Mexico can be serious trouble. I lost precious seconds convincing the guy.

When I finally had him convinced, I brushed aside his apologies and made it out to the street. There was no sign of the man. He had turned the corner, but I couldn't tell which corner. I tried the one to the east. It was the wrong corner. It had started to rain while I had been eating.

It had been cloudy during the evening, but it rains very little there in the desert and I had expected the clouds would simply blow over. Now there was a steady drizzle of rain.

When it rains in the Imperial Valley it makes trouble.

The crops in that fertile soil are predicated upon moisture from irrigation and the ranchers don't want rain. The soil is largely silt from the prehistoric deposits of the Colorado River, and rain turns that soil into a slick clay that is as adhesive as wet paint. Automobile tires spread it over the pavement. It sticks to the soles of the shoes and, on certain surfaces, makes it as difficult to proceed as if one were walking on glare ice.

I went back into the restaurant.

"That man who was just in here saying someone was to have met him—do you know him?" I asked the manager.

"No, señor, I have never seen him before."

"Can you get me a taxi, quick?" I asked.

He went to the door, looked out, looked up at the clouds, looked up and down the street, and shook his head. "Not tonight, I am afraid, señor. This is not like across the border in the United States. Here we usually have one, sometimes two taxicabs. Tonight it is raining and there is none."

Mexico is a wonderful country, but there are some things Mexicans can't understand or don't want to understand. Our hurry and sense of urgency leave them cold.

My man had given me the slip, but I had had a good look at him. I wouldn't forget him.

I had to go to the place where I had left my car, and, it being a rainy evening, there was only one way to get there.

It wasn't too long a walk. I buttoned my coat and made the best of it, keeping under the protection of buildings, porches and awnings wherever possible, and hurrying across the intersections.

Soon I came to the line of cars that was waiting to clear United States Customs at Calexico.

It was a long line.

Overworked immigration men and customs inspectors were at the checking point far up ahead, asking motorists what country they were citizens of, whether they had anything they had bought in Mexico, occasionally putting a sticker on the windshield which meant the car had to pull over out

48

of the line for a detailed search. For the most part, however, after a brief inspection, the cars were waved on.

I'd read up on smuggling, and statistics show that literally tons of marijuana come across the border with a goodly sprinkling of heroin and other contraband mixed in for good measure.

The customs inspectors are unbelievably skillful in sizing up drivers but they are snowed under by the sheer volume of numbers.

Do you know what is the leading tourist city in the world? Rome? Paris? London? Cairo? Guess again. The answer is Tijuana, Baja California, Mexico, and while there aren't nearly as many cars crossing at Mexicali as at Tijuana, the volume is still terrific.

Right now the cars were in a long line, the drivers waiting impatiently with motors running, the windshield wipers beating a monotonous, rhythmic cadence.

I saw a pickup carrying a small houseboat on a trailer and it aroused my curiosity.

Quite a few boating enthusiasts trail their boats down through Mexicali to the fishing port of San Felipe, a hundred and twenty miles to the south. There is a good surfaced road, and fishing and ocean adventure are at the end of it.

Other enthusiasts who are more venturesome go on another fifty-odd miles to the south of San Felipe to Puertecitos, a little gem of a bay, where there are a few dwellings, a few house trailers, supplies, and the warm blue of a gulf which is generally quite tranquil.

A houseboat, however, is something of a novelty.

This one was rather short and was mounted on twin pontoons powered with two outboard motors. The pickup which was pulling the outfit was powerful enough to snake it over roads all the way to Puertecitos if the driver had been so inclined.

49

My eyes came up to the driver and suddenly I snapped to attention. He was the man I was looking for, the one who had been in the Monte Carlo Café a short time before, asking if there was someone there waiting for him, saying that he had been delayed.

I could readily understand the reason for the delay. If he had been fighting his way up from San Felipe over pavement which had suddenly turned wet while he was dragging a pontoon houseboat on a trailer, a delay was to have been expected.

I moved on, just about keeping pace with the slow-moving double line of cars, studying the driver of the pickup.

I noticed that my party had a passenger with him, a male, but I couldn't see much of the man's face because he was on the side away from me and the shadow obscured his features.

Then I crossed the line of traffic and went through the border station myself, giving my citizenship, stating that I had purchased nothing in Mexico.

Again I tried for a taxicab but in vain. I hurried to the point where I had my automobile parked by the side of the road and drove back to the road that led from the border crossing. The pickup with its houseboat had gone. However, I had jotted down the license numbers of both the pickup and the trailer. I felt I could find my man again, although from the description I had of Hale, I knew this man wasn't the one I had been hired to find.

I couldn't be certain about the other man in the pickup, however. He could have been the man I wanted.

I gambled I could follow up the lead I now had.

The rain had got me good and damp.

I finally drove to the Maple Leaf Motel, got a flask out of my suitcase, had a good swig of whiskey and went to sleep.

4

Sometime in the night, when my senses were still drugged with sleep, I was half awakened by the sound of voices raised in what seemed to be an argument.

I rolled over, punched the pillow, went back to sleep again, then suddenly wakened to a realization that those voices *might* have been coming from Unit 12.

It took me a few moments to get my senses together, to jump out of bed and get to the window.

There was no light on in Unit 12.

The voices had ceased.

The motel lay silent under the stars, the night light cast shimmering reflections in the swimming pool in the patio.

I stood by the window until I began to feel chilled. Then I went back to bed, but it was a long while before I could get to sleep. I was lying there listening for the sound of voices, and listening in vain.

I arose at seven o'clock, showered, shaved, and started out to breakfast.

I had a desire for the Mexican dish of *huevos rancheros,* in which fried eggs, swimming in a sauce of onions, peppers and spices, are placed on top of a thin tortilla.

There is no place that makes *huevos rancheros* any better than the kitchen of the De Anza Hotel.

The rain had ceased. The sky was blue, the air clear. It was only a four-block walk to the hotel and I decided to make it, swinging along with shoulders back, inhaling the pure desert air in great, long pulls.

I entered the dining room at the De Anza Hotel, found an inconspicuous table, seated myself, gave my order and sipped delicious coffee while I waited for the eggs to arrive.

The waiter brought the *huevos rancheros.* I put down my coffee cup and looked up into the startled eyes of our client, Milton Carling Calhoun, who was seated three tables away, facing me.

He hadn't expected to see me. His facial expression was a dead giveaway.

I waved to him casually, as though seeing him there was the most natural thing in the world, and went on with my eggs, keeping an eye on him, however, to make sure he didn't sneak out.

He finished before I did and had the grace to come over to my table.

"Well, well, Lam," he said, "good morning. How are you this morning?"

"Fine, thanks. How are you?"

"A little sleepy but very well."

"I hardly expected to see *you* here this morning."

"As a matter of fact," he said, "I hardly expected to be here, but after talking with you over the phone last night I decided to come down so I could . . . could . . . have a chat with you personally. Talking over the telephone is so unsatisfactory."

"Isn't it?" I said.

"Indeed it is."

"Where," I asked, "are you staying?"

"Here in the hotel. It's a very nice place, air-conditioned and all that, and the food is very good."

"You get down here often?" I asked.

"Not often. Now, tell me, Lam, just *what* have you discovered?"

"Not very much more than when I talked with you on the telephone last night."

"But you must have *some* additional facts. You were so secretive last night. I knew I had to *talk* with you. You held out on me on the telephone. You know something else, don't you?"

"Yes."

"What?"

I said, "The young woman is waiting for someone to join her. I think it may be Hale."

"Now, this young woman," Calhoun went on, "you didn't want to mention names over the telephone—that's one reason I wanted to talk with you—just *who* is this young woman?"

"Her name," I said, "is Nanncie Beaver. She's registered here as Nanncie Armstrong. There's a trick spelling on her name. It's N-a-n-n-c-i-e."

"How in the world did you ever get a lead that brought you to her?" he asked.

I said, "I tried to find out all I could about Colburn Hale. I found out that Nanncie was his girl friend, and when I went to look for her I found that she'd mysteriously disappeared at about the same time Colburn Hale had disappeared. It was, therefore, a strong possibility that they were together."

"But how in the world did you ever find her down here?" he asked. "I couldn't—" He broke off suddenly.

"Couldn't what?" I asked.

53

"Couldn't imagine," he said.

"It was routine detective work," I said, "but quite a bit of work at that. What time did you get in here?"

"Around two-thirty or so this morning. It was a mean drive over wet roads."

I said, "Expenses are running up. We make a charge of fifteen cents a mile for the agency car."

"That's all right," he said hastily.

"So," I went on, "the question arises whether you want us to quit when the deposit is used up or whether you want to put up some more money to have us go ahead."

"Go ahead with what?"

"To find Hale, of course."

He took a pencil from his pocket and started playing with it, putting the point on the table, sliding his thumb and forefinger from the eraser down to the point, then upending the pencil and sliding his thumb and forefinger back again. He was thinking of what to tell me, or how to tell me.

I beat him to the punch. "Just why did you want to find Colburn Hale?" I asked.

He hesitated for two or three seconds, then said, "Somehow, Lam, I doubt if that's particularly important."

"It might help if I knew."

"And it might not."

I shrugged my shoulders. "It's your money," I pointed out.

He took out his wallet and extracted two new fifty-dollar bills.

"I'm going to add another hundred dollars to the deposit," he said. "That will take care of things for two more days."

"Not with traveling expenses," I said.

"Well, then, for one more day after the three fifty is used up."

"Okay," I told him, "you're the boss. When this is used up you want me to pack up and go home?"

"If you haven't found him by that time, yes. And make every effort to keep expenses down."

I started to say something, then paused as I regarded the door from the hotel.

The surprise must have shown on my face.

Calhoun, whose back was toward the door, whirled to see what I was looking at.

Sergeant Frank Sellers of the Metropolitan Police saw me at just about that time. His own face registered surprise, although he fought to control the expression. Then he was coming over toward us.

"Well, well, well," he said, "look who's here!"

"Hello, Sergeant, how are you?"

"What are you doing down here, Pint Size?" he asked me. "And who's your friend?"

I said, quickly so that Calhoun would get the idea, "Mr. Calhoun, shake hands with Sergeant Frank Sellers of the Metropolitan Police. Sellers is sort of a liaison man who gets around on cases where outside jurisdictions telephone in for help. Are you down here on official business, Sergeant?"

Sellers grinned and said, "Very neatly done, Donald."

Calhoun extended his hand. Sellers grabbed it, crushed it in his big paw and said, "Pleased to meet you."

"What was neatly done?" I asked.

"Telling Calhoun who I was and warning him that I might be on official business. The way you're acting Calhoun might be a client of yours."

I didn't say anything.

"I am," Calhoun said.

Sellers turned to me. "What's the pitch?" he asked. "What are you doing down here, Pint Size? What does Calhoun want down here?"

"Information," I said.

Sellers pulled up a chair and sat down. "Think I'll join you for a while. You two have had breakfast?"

I nodded. "The *huevos rancheros* here are very good, Sergeant."

"Can't eat 'em," he said. "Have to go pretty easy on spicy food. Now then, let's go back to where we were. You say Calhoun hired you to get information?"

"That's right."

"What sort of information?"

I smiled and said, "You're asking the wrong person. I can't betray the confidences of a client."

Sellers turned to Calhoun. "What sort of information?" he asked.

Calhoun was plainly flabbergasted. "Is this official?" he asked.

"It could be made official," Sellers told him.

Calhoun gave him a long look, then said somewhat coldly, "I fail to see how any stretch of the imagination would make my business with Mr. Lam of any possible interest to you, Sergeant."

Sellers didn't back up an inch. "Then you'd better stretch your imagination some more."

"I've already stretched it to the limit," Calhoun said.

"The name Colburn Hale mean anything to you?" Sellers asked.

Calhoun couldn't resist the slight start.

Sergeant Sellers grinned a triumphant grin.

"I see it does," he said. "Suppose you start talking."

"I don't know what I'm supposed to talk about," Calhoun said.

Sergeant Sellers said, "Now, Pint Size here is a fast worker and you can't underestimate the guy. If you do, you get into trouble. Now, take for instance the case of Marge Fulton who lives at Apartment Forty-two at Eight-seventeen Billinger Street. This man, Colburn Hale, or Cole Hale, as his friends call him, had the apartment next door, Apartment Forty-three.

"Now, what do you think happened? Donald Lam shows up and knocks on the door of Colburn Hale's apartment. He gets no answer. So then he knocks again until finally Marge Fulton comes to the door of her apartment to see what the noise is all about and to tell Donald Lam that she doesn't think Hale is home.

"Now, that's where you can't underestimate this guy. He's ingenious. He leads Marge Fulton to think he's Colburn Hale's agent. He pumps her for all she knows—which is that Hale moved out in the middle of the night. Then Pint Size shows up down here."

Calhoun looked from Sergeant Sellers to me, then back to Sellers.

"And," Sellers went on, "Donald Lam somehow got information that put him on the track of coming down here to the border. So we'd like to know a little bit more about Hale and just what your interest is in the guy."

"Is he hot?" I asked.

Sellers measured his words carefully. "He may be hot and he may be cold—very cold."

I said, "The Calexico Police Department didn't telephone for help just because someone in Los Angeles is missing."

"That's logical," Sellers agreed affably.

"And," I said, "if you were looking for Hale and you knew I'd been looking for him, you must have uncovered a lead which brought you down here without knowing you were on my back trail because you were surprised when you walked into the dining room here this morning and saw me."

"Who says so?" Sellers asked.

"Your face said so."

Sellers said, "We're getting our roles mixed. I'm doing the questioning."

"Has any crime been committed?" I asked.

"Could be," Sellers said. "Hale is mixed up in a dope-running case. We don't know how deep."

I said to Calhoun, "In that case, if any crime has been committed and if there's any reason to suspect you of any connection with the crime, you don't have to say a word. Sellers has to warn you that anything you say can be used against you and that you're entitled to the advice of an attorney."

"But there *can't* be any crime involved," Calhoun said.

"Oh, sure," I said sarcastically. "Frank Sellers just came down here to sell tickets to the Policemen's Ball."

Sellers grinned.

After a few moments of silence, Sellers said, "Now I'll start telling both of you jokers something. I flew down here in a police plane. I didn't get in until after five o'clock this morning, but I had some pretty good leads. I went right to work.

"Hale was a writer. He did all sorts of things, little short articles, fiction, and, occasionally, he'd run onto some article that he could sell to the wire services.

"Now, somewhere along the line he found out something about the marijuana traffic. He had been investigating that quietly and under cover for some little time. He evidently stumbled onto something big because the night he disappeared he was pounding like mad on his typewriter.

"Then something happened. Some man came to see him. We want to know more about that. Who was that man, a friend or an enemy?

"Hale packed up and got out. He evidently didn't have too much junk, but what he had he threw into an automobile, and the guy vanished.

"Now, that could have meant either one of two things. Either he had a lot of red-hot information that he was going to spill in an article on marijuana smuggling, the word got around and some friend of his came to tip him off that the situation was hot and he'd better get out, so he got out, or he knew a shipment was coming across, and he came to the border.

"The fact that he took all of his things with him makes me think that it was a friend that gave him the tip.

"On the other hand, it could have been that it was an enemy, some member of the dope ring.

"Hale was busily engaged in typing out a story that was red-hot and there was a knock at the door. He went to open the door and found himself looking down the barrel of a gun.

"The man behind that gun just took Hale with him and wanted to be awfully careful that he didn't leave anything behind in the way of notes, so he and a couple of buddies cleaned out the apartment.

"Right now," Sellers said, "we're acting on the theory that Hale's move was voluntary, that he hadn't all of his article finished, that he suddenly realized he was hot, that some friend came and helped him and they moved in a hurry.

"Now then, we'd like . . ."

The door opened and a man who had police officer stamped all over him came into the dining room, looked around, saw Sellers, pounded over to him and touched him on the shoulder. "Can I speak with you a minute, Sergeant?" he asked.

Sellers looked up. "Why, sure," he said.

The two officers walked over to a corner of the dining room where they were out of earshot. The local officer poured stuff into Sellers' ears and Sellers was jolted—there was no question about that.

Whatever the local guy told him was important enough so that Sellers never came back. The two men walked out of the room and Sellers didn't even so much as give us a backward glance over his shoulder.

Calhoun said, "Gosh, *that* was close!"

I watched the door through which the officers had disappeared. After a few thoughtful seconds, I turned back to Calhoun. "That brief interlude," I said, "gives you a chance to start talking."

"To whom about what?"

"To me about you."

"I don't think you need to know any more than you know already."

"Think again," I told him.

He hesitated for a moment, then said, "Colburn Hale really is nothing to me."

"Sure," I said sarcastically. "You toss three hundred and fifty dollars onto Bertha Cool's desk to try to find him and then you put another hundred into the kitty down here, but he's less than nothing to you."

Calhoun looked at me thoughtfully, then said, "I'm going to tell you the truth."

"It just might make a welcome change," I pointed out.

He said, "I'm not interested in Colburn Hale. I'm interested in Nanncie Beaver."

He jolted me with that one. "What?" I asked.

"That's right," he said. "I'm interested in Nanncie Beaver. She ran away with every evidence of having left in a panic. I tried to trace her. There wasn't a chance. So I went to see if Colburn Hale had anything to do with her disappearance and I found out that Hale had left very hurriedly. I figured they were both together.

"I didn't want anyone to know I was interested in Nanncie Beaver. I didn't even dare to tell you and Bertha Cool, but I felt if you could locate Colburn Hale, that would give me all the information I needed to find Nanncie."

"Why be so secretive?" I asked.

Calhoun said, "Because I'm married. It's not a happy marriage. We're getting a divorce. My wife and I are working out a property settlement right now through our lawyers. I can't afford to play into her hands. If she knew anything about Nanncie Beaver the fat would be in the fire. Her demands for a settlement would go way up out of all reason."

I said, "If you had put the cards on the table with us you might have saved yourself a lot of time and a lot of money."

"Then, by the same token," he said, "you or Bertha Cool might have made a slip and it could have cost me two or three hundred . . ."

"Two or three hundred thousand?" I asked, finishing the sentence for him.

He thought for a moment, then said, "Could be."

I did a lot of thinking. "Look," I said, "you've lied to me about a lot of things. You drove down here and you went directly to Unit Twelve at the Maple Leaf Motel when you arrived. You had to talk with Nanncie. There was an argument. Things didn't go as smoothly as you expected."

"What makes you think that?" he asked.

"You forget that I'm in Unit Seven," I said. "I was awake by voices last night, voices coming from Unit Twelve."

"You heard voices?" he asked.

"Voices."

"A man and a woman?"

"That's right."

"Did you hear what was being said?"

I said, "Suppose you quit asking me questions for a while and start telling me the facts. You may be in this thing a little deeper than you anticipate."

"I've told you the facts."

I shook my head. "No, you haven't."

"What do you mean by that?"

I said, "If you had really been anxious to locate Nanncie when I told you last night over the telephone that I'd followed her down here and that she was in Unit Twelve of the Maple Leaf Motel, you'd have said, 'Well, I've gone as far as I want to go with this thing, Lam. I've spent all the money I can afford to spend, and if you haven't located Colburn Hale by this time, you'd better come on home and call it a day.'

"Instead of that you jump in your car and come down here and when you see me this morning you fork over another hundred bucks first thing."

"Well, what does that prove?" he asked, trying to be belligerent.

I said, "It proves that your actions and your words don't fit together."

I pushed back my chair. "Come on," I said, "let's go see Nanncie."

"I . . . I don't want to see her now."

"You're going to see her now," I said.

"You're working for me," he pointed out.

"You're damn right I am, and there's more to this than meets the eye, otherwise Sergeant Sellers wouldn't be down here. Come on, we're going to see Nanncie."

"I don't want to see her now."

"I'm going to see her now. You can come along if you want to have it that way, or you can stay here."

"All right," he said, "I'll come along."

I paid the check and left a tip.

"Where's your car?" I asked.

"Parked out front."

"Let's go in it. Time may be a little more precious than we realize."

It was a big Cadillac and we purred the four blocks to the

Maple Leaf Motel, found a parking place, got out and approached Unit Twelve.

The key was in the door on the outside.

"What does that mean?" Calhoun asked.

"It probably means that she's checked out," I said.

"She couldn't have."

"Why not?" I asked.

He was silent at that one.

I walked up to the door, bold as brass, and knocked on it. When I received no answer, I pulled the door open.

The bed had been slept in but hadn't been made. I went into the bathroom. There was a bathmat on the floor, but it was dry. The bath towels were folded on the rack. They were both dry.

We looked the place over. There wasn't any sign of baggage or any article of women's clothing.

"Okay," I said to Calhoun, "let's get out of here. We'll go to my place. Perhaps you can refresh your memory there and tell me a bit more."

5

Calhoun and I went into Unit 7.

The bed hadn't been made. I put a couple of pillows behind my back and sat on the bed, giving Calhoun the only comfortable chair in the place.

"Well?" I said.

"Well, what?"

"Some more talk," I told him.

He shook his head. He was worried. "Lam," he said, "I can't afford to have my name mixed up in this thing. Good Lord, if there's any publicity and my wife should get hold of it—that lawyer of hers is a vulture. He picks the last shred of meat off the smallest bone he can find. This little escapade alone could cost me a . . . well, plenty."

I said, "You don't need to talk to anyone except me."

"If I don't talk, they'll throw newspaper publicity all over me."

"If you do talk, what'll they do?" I asked.

He didn't like the answer to that one either.

We sat for a couple of minutes in silence. I was thinking and Calhoun was worrying.

The door pushed open and Sellers came in.

"Well?" he asked.

I tried to look innocent.

"Start talking," Sellers said.

"What happened to your friend?" I asked.

"He's a deputy sheriff," Sellers said. "He's been called away on business." He looked at me, grinned, and said, "Important business. Maybe you know what it is."

I shook my head.

"Talk," Sellers said.

I said, "Calhoun and I are going on a fishing trip down to San Felipe when you get done bullying us around. I did a little job for him and he was very grateful. He offered to meet me here this morning and we'd go down to San Felipe together and try to catch some fish. He's giving the party."

"And what was the little job you did for your friend here?" Sellers asked.

I said, "Calhoun is planning an exposé on drug traffic from Mexico. Colburn Hale has some material he wanted to get. Hale left overnight. My client wanted to find him."

"And what brought you down here?" Sellers asked. "Go ahead, Pint Size, better think fast because you haven't time to think up a really good one and I'm going to trap you on any lies you tell. When that happens you and Bertha are going to be in serious trouble.

"We're investigating a crime. You know what happens to people who give false information to officers who are investigating a crime."

"What sort of a crime?" I asked.

"Murder one," Sellers said.

I came bolt upright on the bed. "Murder what?"

"Murder one, you heard me."

"Who's the victim? Is it Hale?"

"Nope," Sellers said, "it's a chap by the name of Eddie Sutton. The name mean anything to you, Pint Size?"

I shook my head. "Not a thing."

"Sutton," Sellers said, "is part of a smuggling ring. They're pretty slick.

"We hadn't found out just how they worked until this morning. Sutton posed as an enthusiastic yachtsman. He had a little houseboat on pontoons that he'd trail back and forth from San Felipe, sometimes down as far south as Puertecitos.

"Last night Sutton came back from San Felipe and checked through the border here a little after nine forty-five—perhaps as late as ten-fifteen—that's as nearly as we can place it. He got through the border without any trouble. He got out to the outskirts of Calexico here and pulled off to the side of the road.

"We think a scout car was waiting to join him. That scout car was to go ahead and make sure the coast was clear. It would have had a Citizen's Band radio.

"Last night there was a roadblock traffic check just this side of Brawley. The way we figure it, the scout car radioed back to Sutton.

"Sutton decided to hole up. He went back into the houseboat.

"He never came out."

"Why?" I asked.

"On account of a bullet through the heart," Sellers said. "We think it's probably a thirty-eight caliber."

"When was his body found?"

"About seven o'clock this morning."

"How long had he been dead?"

Sellers shrugged his shoulders. "Maybe three hours, maybe seven hours."

"Why tell us all this?" I asked.

"Because," Sellers said, "I think that perhaps you can help us, and, in case you can't, we'll give you the facts so that you'll know we're investigating a murder case. Then if you do uncover anything you'll know the consequences of withholding the information."

Sellers pulled a cigar from his pocket, ripped off the end with his teeth, shoved the cigar in his mouth, but didn't light it. He stood there looking at us with a sardonic gleam in his eye.

"Now then," he said, "you two are going to take a little ride with me."

"Official?" I asked.

"We can make it official."

I got up off the bed and said to Calhoun, "Let's go."

"Where are we going?" Calhoun asked.

"Down to the police parking lot," Sellers said.

"What for?"

"I want you to take a look at the scene of the crime."

I said, "I may be able to help you, Sergeant."

Sellers pulled the cigar out of his mouth, inspected the wet place and grinned. "I thought perhaps you'd break loose with a little information."

"It's not the kind you think," I said. "It has nothing to do with my reason for being here."

"No?"

"No."

"Well, tell me," Sellers said, putting the cigar back in the right-hand side of his mouth and twisting it over to the left side by rolling it with his tongue.

I said, "I was coming across the border last night on foot and I saw this outfit coming through, at least it's an outfit that matches the description you gave me—a small house-boat on pontoons being carried on a trailer."

67

"What time?" Sellers asked.

"I can't give it to you any better than you have it already. It was somewhere, I would say, between nine forty-five and ten-fifteen. When I last saw it, it was about ten o'clock."

"Anything else?" Sellers asked.

I said, "The man who was driving the pickup had parked the outfit someplace within easy walking distance of the Monte Carlo Café, went into the café and looked around to see if he could find somebody who was going to meet him there."

"The devil!" Sellers said.

I nodded.

"How do you know?"

"I was in the café."

"Anything else?"

"Yes," I said. "The guy wasn't alone."

"You mean someone was with him when he came in the café?"

"No, someone was in the pickup with him when he crossed the border."

Sellers' eyes narrowed. He bit several times on the end of the cigar, chewing it gently while he digested that bit of information.

"Description," he said.

"I can't give it to you."

"Why not?"

"It was dark. I was walking across the border. This pickup was in the line that was waiting to go across. I got a good look at the driver, but the man with him was on the side of the car away from me and was in the deeper shadows."

"Any idea how tall, how old, how heavy?"

"I'd say he was probably somewhere in his thirties, but that's just making a blind stab at it from the set of his shoulders and the way he held his head. I don't know how tall he'd have been if he'd been standing up, but when he was sitting he was about average height."

"Come on," Sellers said. "I'm going to show you jokers something."

We followed him out to a police car. He took us to a parking lot by the police station.

"This the outfit?" Sellers asked, when we got out and faced a pontoon houseboat mounted on a trailer pulled by a Ford pickup.

"That's the outfit."

"Well, you can't go in," Sellers said. "We're going through it with a fine-tooth comb, looking for fingerprints and clues, but I want to show you guys something."

He led us over to the rear part of one of the pontoons.

I could see this had already been processed for fingerprints. There was dusting powder over it and a couple of good latents which had evidently already been photographed.

Sellers said, "Just a minute." He picked up two metal bottle openers that were on a stool by the end of the pontoon, fitted the two bent ends to a little ridge on the pontoon and pulled.

The cap loosened.

Sellers took his handkerchief so he wouldn't leave any fingerprints and took the end completely off.

The pontoon underneath was filled with dried marijuana that had been stuffed in and packed until it was solid.

I gave a low whistle.

Calhoun said nothing.

Sellers said, "As you can see, we got a couple of good fingerprints off the tip here. Now then, just to protect yourselves, I think it will be a good idea if you'll just step inside the station with me and leave your fingerprints."

"Why?"

"We just want to make sure that the latents we have developed aren't the prints of either one of you."

I looked at Calhoun.

"I don't think you have any right to take our prints under the circumstances," Calhoun said.

"Probably not," Sellers said, "but I think we're going to take them just the same—one way or another. What's the matter, you got any objections?"

"None at all," I said hastily. "As a matter of fact, you've got mine on file. You've taken them several times."

"I know, I know," Sellers said.

Calhoun said, "This is an arbitrary high-handed procedure. If you had the faintest reason to suspect either one of us it would be different, but you're just on a general fishing expedition and—"

"And," Sellers interrupted him, studying him with a cold, speculative eye, "we've been looking you up, Mr. Milton Carling Calhoun.

"You and your wife are separated. Since the separation you have been living in the Mantello Apartments, a very swanky apartment out on Wilshire Boulevard.

"Around nine-thirty last night you got a call from Mexicali which came through the apartment switchboard. Right after that you phoned the apartment garage, told the attendant you had to have your car right away, that you were being called out of town on a business trip.

"Evidently the call gave you information which was important enough so you left immediately for the Imperial Valley. You must have arrived about two o'clock this morning. It must have been rather a tough trip because of the rain. I thought you looked a little tired when I met you.

"You know, you must have driven right past this houseboat where it was parked by the side of the road when you came into town. You might have recognized the outfit, I don't know. You may have stopped and gone inside. We're finding a few fingerprints on the inside as well as these on the outside on the cover of the pontoons.

"Now, Mr. Milton Carling Calhoun, would you like to step inside and have your fingerprints taken?"

Calhoun took a long breath. "How in the world did you find out about the telephone call and the time I left Los Angeles?"

Sellers grinned around the cigar. "Don't underestimate the police, son. I put through a long-distance call after I talked with you at breakfast and had the information I wanted within a matter of minutes. You are very law-abiding. When you changed your residence, you even notified the Department of Motor Vehicles of your new address—it's very commendable. That's the law, you know. Now, that Mantello Apartments is a swanky outfit. They have a twenty-four-hour switchboard service. The night operator didn't listen in on your call, but she remembers that it came from Mexicali. Do you suppose there's any chance that it was Eddie Sutton who was calling you to tell he'd reached the border okay with his shipment and you told him to park the outfit and wait until you got there?"

"You're crazy," Calhoun said.

Sellers pulled the soggy end of the cigar out of his mouth, inspected the frayed end which he had chewed, put the cigar back in his mouth, pulled out a lighter, snapped it into flame and held the flame at the end of the cigar until a cold, bluish-white whisp of smoke made its appearance.

"So far I haven't anything to go on except hunches," he said. "But I'm playing hunches. Come on in and we'll take your fingerprints."

We went inside and Sellers took our fingerprints.

It was evidently the first time Calhoun had had all of his fingerprints taken. He was a little awkward, and the finger-

71

print technician had to hold the tip of each finger firmly as he gently rotated the finger. He also fumbled around a little when it came to handling the paper tissue with the ink solvent on it which the technician handed him.

Sellers puffed on the cigar.

"All right, you two," he said, "I'll take you back to the motel. Be sure to let me know if you think of anything else."

6

When Sellers had driven away, I said to Calhoun, "Suppose you come clean with me."

"I'm already clean with you," he said irritably. "You talk like that damn Los Angeles cop."

I said, "All right, I'll ask a few questions. Why did you want to find Hale?"

"I've told you why. Because I wanted to look for Nanncie."

"And why did you want to find Nanncie?"

"Because I knew she was getting mixed into a very dangerous situation."

"This man, Hale, was a rival of yours?"

"With a girl as good-looking as Nanncie, everybody is a potential rival."

"And how did you know Hale was working on a dope story?"

"Because Nanncie told me."

"She betrayed Hale's confidence?"

"It wasn't his confidence. Nanncie was the one who had lined up the story for him in the first place."

"And where did Nanncie get it?"

"She got a tip from an operator in a beauty shop and followed up on the story."

"Why? Because she was interested in dope?"

"No, because she was interested in Hale. She knew he was looking for something that would make a sensational article and she thought this would be it. It was a man's story."

"Did she have details?"

"I don't know."

"Don't pull that line with me. You and Nanncie were pretty close. If she told you anything, she told you all. Did she say anything about a houseboat on a trailer?"

Calhoun didn't answer that question for a second or two, then he said, "I'm not going to have you cross-examine me this way, Lam."

I said, "You damn fool, I'm trying to save your bacon. You've left a broad back trail. Don't underestimate the police. Frank Sellers is going after Nanncie."

"And we've got to go after her," Calhoun said.

"He'll pick her up somewhere," I said. "She didn't have a car. She probably didn't take a taxi. Somebody came and picked her up, probably about three or four o'clock this morning. That was shortly after you had arrived in Calexico. I think you did it."

"You think wrong," Calhoun said. "I only wish to heaven I had been the one. I'd have taken her and put her in a safe place."

"Safe for whom?" I asked. "You or her?"

"Her."

"I'm still not sure you didn't pick her up," I told him. "Now, we'll come back to the original question. Did she tell you anything about a houseboat that was used in the smuggling operation?"

"Well, generally."

"So when you drove into town in the wee small hours of the morning and saw a pickup with a pontoon houseboat on a trailer parked by the side of the road, what did you do?"

"All right," he said. "I thought—well, I didn't know what to think. I stopped the car and went across to try to get in the door of the houseboat."

"What did you do?"

"I knocked."

"And you left fingerprints."

"Knuckles don't leave fingerprints."

I said, "What were you intending to do if the guy had opened the door—ask him if he was the dope peddler that your girl friend, Nanncie, had been telling you about?"

"No, I was going to sound him out a bit, pretending I was a yachtsman and wanted information about launching facilities at San Felipe."

"At three o'clock in the morning?" I asked.

"I tell you I was worried sick about Nanncie," he said. "I wasn't thinking clearly."

"And you're not thinking clearly now," I told him, then I asked him abruptly, "Do you own a gun?"

He hesitated, then nodded.

"Where is it?"

"I . . . why, home, I guess."

"Where is home? Where your wife is living on in the Mantello Apartments?"

"In the . . . in the home, I guess."

"You sure?"

"No, I'm not absolutely certain. I haven't seen it for some time."

"What is it?"

"A thirty-eight-caliber revolver."

"You're sure you didn't bring it with you when you came down here last night?"

"No, certainly not. Why would I have brought it?"

"Sometimes people carry guns when they're traveling at night over lonely roads in an automobile."

"I don't. I'm law-abiding."

"All right," I said. "The best thing for you to do is to go back to Los Angeles."

"Are you crazy?" he asked. "I've got to stay down here and together we've got to look for Nanncie."

"Not together."

"I want to be kept posted. I want to know what you're doing. I want to work with you."

"You would simply clutter up the scenery," I told him.

"I have reason to believe she's in danger."

"If she is, I can help her a lot better if I'm alone than if you're hanging around. What are your feelings toward Colburn Hale. I want to know."

"I hate him," he said.

"Jealous?"

"I'm not jealous. I just tell you that the man dragged Nanncie into danger, fooling around with this article of his on dope smuggling."

I told Calhoun, "If you won't go back to Los Angeles, there's just one thing I want you to do."

"What?"

"Get in that Cadillac of yours, drive to the De Anza Hotel, go into your room, close the door, don't do any telephoning, and stay put."

"For how long—I'd go crazy."

"Until you hear from me," I said.

"How long will that be?"

"It depends."

"On what?"

"On when I can find some of the answers."

"Answers to what?"

76

I looked him straight in the eyes and said, "Answers to some of the things you've been doing and have lied about."

"What do you mean by that?"

"I mean that I have a feeling you're not being frank with me."

"I've paid you everything you've asked. You're working for me."

"That's right," I told him, "and if you want to keep me running around in circles like a trotting horse that's being trained at the end of a rope, that's your privilege. I'll trot around just as far as you want and as fast as you want at fifty bucks a day and expenses.

"On the other hand, if you want to take the rope off my neck and let me trot straight down the road so I can get somewhere, I'll try to get somewhere."

"Perhaps then you'd get to some place that I don't want you to be."

"There's always that chance."

"I can't take it."

"You can if you tell me where you *don't* want me to go," I said, "and why you don't want me to get there."

He shook his head.

I said, "Has it ever occurred to you that you could find yourself charged with murder?"

"With murder?"

"With murder in the first," I said. "Sellers is measuring you for size right now. A fingerprint or two or just some little bit of evidence and you'd be elected."

"Why, they couldn't . . . they wouldn't dare."

"And," I said, "there'd be nice, juicy big headlines in the papers. LOS ANGELES MILLIONAIRE ARRESTED IN DOPE-SMUG-GLING MURDER."

He acted as though I'd hit him in the stomach.

"Think it over," I told him. "I'm trying to help you. Despite

77

all the double crosses you've given me, I'm still trying to help, but there are certain things I can't do. I can't suppress evidence. And when I know that the police are investigating a murder case, I can't lie to them. After all, I'm a licensed private detective and I have certain obligations under the law.

"Now get out of here. Go to the De Anza Hotel. Shut yourself in your room and stay there."

He looked at me as a wounded deer looks at the hunter. Then he got up and walked out.

7

I didn't have much trouble finding where the houseboat had been parked. I drove slowly out of town, watching the road.

There was still a little crowd hanging around, enough people so that it was impossible to tell anything about footprints or wheel tracks. The police had apparently roped the place off earlier in the morning, and after they finished with their search and photography they had taken the ropes away, presumably when they moved the pickup and trailer. Then the people had moved in.

I looked the place over.

It was a real wide space on the west side of the road, which would be the left-hand side going north. It must have been a good fifty feet from the edge of the pavement over to a drainage ditch that was along the side of the road. On the other side of the drainage ditch was a barbed-wire fence and beyond that was an alfalfa field.

As the alfalfa field was irrigated, the surplus waters ran

down into the drainage ditch, which was still moist with a base of muddy clay on the bottom.

I walked along the road, looking at the drainage ditch to see if I could see any footprints.

There weren't any in it, but there were lots of them along the side. The police, and presumably some of the spectators, had looked to see if anyone had crossed that ditch. It couldn't have been done without leaving a set of tracks.

I took off my shoes and socks and waded through the clay mud in the bottom of the ditch, climbed the bank on the other side, and crawled through the barbed-wire fence, holding my shoes and socks in my left hand, trying to act natural and unconcerned—just a loco gringo doing something that didn't make sense.

I walked about fifty yards along the bank, looking over in the alfalfa field; and then I walked back to where I had started and walked fifty yards in the other direction.

I started back, and then I saw it, a gleam of bluish metal reflecting the sunlight.

I glanced around. Everyone seemed to have lost interest in me.

I walked through the alfalfa field for about twenty feet.

The gun was lying at the foot of an alfalfa plant.

I studied it intently. It was a blued-steel .38-caliber, snub-nosed revolver.

I turned and walked slowly away from what I had found.

I had taken only a few steps toward the fence when a little ten-year-old, black-eyed, barefooted urchin came running across the muddy bottom of the drainage ditch.

"What did you find, mister?" he asked.

"Find?" I echoed, trying to look innocent.

"You found something. You moved over. You . . . I'll look."

He started to run back to where I had turned into the alfalfa.

"Wait!" I called after him.

He stopped.

"I found something," I said, "that is of great importance. I don't want the other people to know. Can I trust you?"

His face showed intense excitement. "Of course, sure," he said. "What do you want?"

I said, "I am going to wait here to see that what I found is not disturbed. I was going to call the police myself, but it is better this way. You have your mother and father near here?"

"I live in that house over there," he said, pointing. "The white house."

"Do you have a telephone?"

"Yes."

I said, "I'll wait here. Don't say anything to any of the people out there. Go to your house. Get your father if he is home, your mother if he isn't home. Telephone the Calexico police. Tell them to get out here right away, that Donald Lam has found some important evidence."

"A Lam?" he asked.

"Donald Lam," I said. "L-a-m. You think you can do that?"

"Oh, sure."

"And don't say anything to anybody except your parents."

"Only my mother," he said. "My father is at work."

"Then hurry," I told him.

I sat down on the bank of the ditch and waited while the kid wormed his way through the barbed-wire fence, spattered across the muddy bottom of the ditch, and, with his bare brown feet beating an excited tattoo on the ground, headed off for the big white house.

It took about fifteen minutes for Frank Sellers and a Calexico cop to get there.

The kid was waiting for them. He beckoned them eagerly and led the way across the ditch.

Sellers and the cop hesitated before getting in the mud, but finally they waded on through.

The people who had been aimlessly milling around suddenly became interested when they saw the cops' car and the ten-year-old kid leading the two men across the drainage ditch. Then they noticed me and one or two came trooping across, but the officer waved them back before they got into the alfalfa field.

Sellers and the officer came slogging down to me.

"This had better be good, Pint Size," Sellers said.

"Want to take a look?" I asked.

I led the way and stopped when I reached a point where they could see the gun.

"I'll be go to hell!" Sellers said.

They looked at each other; then they looked at me. "Have you been over there?" Sellers asked.

"This is as close as I've been."

"I hope you're telling the truth," Sellers said. "How did you know that gun was there?"

"I didn't. I came out to look the place over."

"Lots of people have looked the place over," Sellers said.

"I reasoned that if a man wanted to get rid of a gun, he'd stand on the edge of that drainage ditch and throw it out into the field, just as far as he could throw it."

"Why not take it with him for a ways and throw it where it wouldn't be found."

"He might not have had that much time. The gun was too incriminating. He wanted to get rid of it right now."

"All right, Pint Size," Sellers said, "you masterminded that, but what caused you to cross the ditch?"

"Because no one else had crossed the ditch," I said.

"How did you know that?"

"No one could have crossed the ditch without leaving tracks."

"And so?" Sellers asked.

"So I knew that no one had looked in the alfalfa field."

"And how did you know the gun was in the alfalfa field?"

"I didn't, but as a matter of good investigative technique I knew that all the terrain around the scene of the crime should be explored, particularly places where a weapon could have been thrown."

Sellers looked at the Calexico cop, took a cigar from his pocket and put it in his mouth, walked over to the gun, bent slowly down, took a fountain pen from his pocket, inserted it in the barrel and lifted the gun.

"The chances of latent fingerprints on a gun are pretty slim," he said, "but we'll just protect this evidence as much as we can and dust it for fingerprints."

"For my money," the Calexico cop said, "you'll find the fingerprints of this slick detective."

Sellers shook his head. "We may find it's been wiped clean of fingerprints, but he's too slick to pull a boob trick like that."

We walked back along the bank of the ditch, Sellers holding the gun up in the air, the fountain pen in the barrel, keeping it from falling.

He had some trouble getting through the fence and holding the gun, looking like a Japanese juggler trying to hold a ball aloft on a billiard cue.

By this time the crowd had gathered in a big semicircle, gaping at the officers and the gun.

The officers slogged across the muddy bottom of the drainage ditch. I walked across barefoot and over to where I had parked my car.

"Don't try to get lost," Sellers warned. "We may want you."

"You can always find me," I told him. "Unit Seven, Maple Leaf Motel, or somewhere in the vicinity."

"You're right," Sellers said, "we can always find you. I just hope it won't be too much trouble."

I got back in my car and tried to drive barefooted. It was too ticklish.

I stopped at the first service station, got out, and turned the water hose on my feet. The attendant looked at me with a baffled expression.

"I got my feet dirty," I told him.

He shook his head. "Now I've seen everything," he said.

I didn't try to put my socks on over my wet feet. I simply put my shoes on and drove back to the De Anza Hotel, found that Milton Carling Calhoun was in Room 36B, found the room and knocked on the door.

Calhoun opened the door eagerly.

His face showed disappointment when he saw who it was. "You again!" he said.

"Me again," I told him.

My feet were dry by this time. I walked in and sat down in a chair, pulling my socks from my pocket. I took off my shoes and put my socks on.

"Now what," Calhoun asked, "is the idea?"

"I went out to the scene of the crime," I said.

"You mean the murder?"

"What other crime is there?"

"Dope smuggling."

"It was the same scene," I said.

"What happened?" he wanted to know.

I said, "The cops pulled a boner."

"How come?"

I grinned and said, "Sergeant Sellers came down here from Los Angeles. He's the high-powered liaison guy, the expert on homicide investigation, and he pulled a boner right in front of all these local cops. I'll bet he feels like two cents right now."

"What did he do?"

"He failed to search the scene of the crime for a weapon."

"You mean they hadn't . . . ?"

"Oh, they'd looked the trailer over and they'd looked the ground over all around the trailer," I said, "but there was an alfalfa field and a ditch with a muddy bottom between the edge of the highway right-of-way and the field. If anybody had tried to cross over they'd have left tracks.

"The officers looked the place over, found there were no tracks, so assumed no one had been over to the alfalfa field and they could cross it off the books."

"And what happened?" Calhoun asked.

I said, "You should always search the premises, not only the immediate premises, but look at places where a person could stand and throw some object such as a weapon that he wanted to get rid of."

"You mean there was a weapon?" Calhoun asked.

"There was a weapon," I said. "A thirty-eight-caliber revolver, blued-steel, snub-nosed—it looked to me like an expensive gun. The police took it into custody and, of course, got on the telephone right away.

"Within a matter of minutes they'll have found the sales record of the gun from the numbers. Then they'll process it for fingerprints—probably they won't have much luck with that. Latent fingerprints aren't usually found on a gun."

"But they can identify it from the numbers?"

"Sure," I said. "There's a sales record on every gun. Now, is there any chance this is your gun?"

He shook his head emphatically. "Not one chance in a thousand. I know where my gun is."

"Where?"

He hesitated, then said, "Home."

"Let's do better than that," I said. "You may not know it, but you're a poor liar."

He took a deep breath and said, "All right, Nanncie has it."

"How do you know?"

"Because I gave it to her. The poor kid was worried sick and she was scared. I didn't know she was going to try to run away. I thought she was going to stick it out . . . I told her, 'Nanncie, when you go to bed, keep your door locked and don't open it for anybody unless you know for sure who it is. Keep this gun under your pillow and if you have to use it, don't hesitate to do so.'"

"And then?" I asked.

"And then I showed her how to pull the trigger," he said. "You know, it's a self-cocking gun. It sometimes takes a little practice for a woman to pull the trigger so she can fire the gun."

"And you think Nanncie has hung onto the gun?"

"I know she has."

"What are the chances," I asked, "that Nanncie got involved in this thing and pulled the trigger on the gun out there in the trailer?"

"Not a chance in the world," he said. "Not a chance in a million."

I thought it over and said, "Well, maybe you're right. I'm basing my judgment on the fact that she didn't have an automobile and she'd hardly have hired a taxicab to follow the dope car up to the place where the crime was committed, then told the taxi to wait while she went in, pulled a gun and got rid of Eddie Sutton."

"You talk like a fish," Calhoun said impatiently. "Nanncie wouldn't have—"

Imperative knuckles sounded on the door.

I said, wearily, "You'd better open the door for Sergeant Sellers."

Calhoun opened the door.

Sellers took one look at me and said, "Well, well, Pint Size, I see you hotfooted it up here to tell your client the news."

"I've told him the news," I said.

Sellers said to Calhoun, "You own a Smith and Wesson thirty-eight-caliber revolver with a one-and-seven-eighths-inch barrel, number one-three-three-three-four-seven. Where is it?"

"Go ahead and answer the question," I told Calhoun. "He's now suspecting you of a specific crime and asking you a specific incriminating question. He hasn't warned you of your constitutional rights, and anything you say can't be used against you . . ."

Sergeant Sellers resorted to profanity, fished the Miranda card out of his pocket.

The Miranda card is something that officers carry these days since the decision of the United States Supreme Court in the Miranda case. They have to give a series of warnings to anyone, either when they're making an arrest or when the investigation has quit being an investigation in general terms and has moved into a specific area where they are questioning a specific suspect about a specific crime.

Sellers started reading.

"You are," Sellers droned in a monotone, "under suspicion of having murdered one Edward Sutton. You are warned that anything you say may be used against you. On the other hand, you are advised that you do not need to make any statement at all. You are also advised that you are entitled to consult an attorney of your own choice and to have an attorney represent you at all stages of the investigation. If you are unable to afford an attorney, the state will get one to represent you."

Sellers put the card back in his pocket. "Now then," he said, "when did you last see this gun?"

I said to Calhoun, "You're entitled to have an attorney at all stages of the proceeding. Do you have a lawyer?"

"Not here," Calhoun said.

"Suppose you keep out of this," Sellers advised me.

"You mean he's not entitled to have an attorney?" I asked.

"I've already told him," Sellers said, "he's entitled to have an attorney."

I caught Calhoun's eye and surreptitiously put my finger to my tightly closed lips.

Calhoun said, "I have no statement to make. I want to consult a lawyer."

"You may call a lawyer," Sellers said.

Calhoun gulped, thought, then suddenly turned to me. "Lam," he said, "I want a lawyer."

"Don't you have one in—"

"Not one that would be any good in a situation of this sort," he said. "I want a local lawyer and I want the best lawyer in the county—the best *criminal* lawyer."

Calhoun reached in his pocket, pulled out his billfold and started counting out fifty-dollar bills; then he changed his mind, looked in the other side of the billfold and pulled out five one-hundred-dollar bills. He handed them to me. "Three hundred is for you," he said. "Two hundred is for a retainer for the lawyer. Get him to come to the jail and talk with me. I'll make arrangements for his fee then.

"In the meantime, you go ahead and keep working on this case. I'm well able to pay at the price we agreed upon."

"There will be expenses," I said.

"Incur them."

"Where do I stop?" I asked. "What's the limit?"

Calhoun pointed upward. "The sky is the limit."

Sellers said, "I hate to do this to you, Calhoun. If you would cooperate with us, it might not be necessary to take you into custody. After all, we simply are trying to find out about the gun and to trace your movements."

Calhoun looked at me. I shook my head.

"You aren't his lawyer, Pint Size!" Sellers said irritably. "You don't need to advise him."

"I'm his investigator," I said.

"Then you'd better be damn certain you keep your nose clean or we'll give you an adjoining cell. Then you can do all the yakety-yakking you want to."

"With both cells wired for sound," I said.

"You're damn right we'll have them bugged," Sellers said angrily. "How simple do you think we are?"

"You'd be surprised," I told him.

Sellers turned to Calhoun. "I'm not going to put handcuffs on you under the circumstances, but you're under arrest and don't make any mistake about it. Don't make any false moves. Come on, let's go."

They got to the door and we went out. Calhoun locked the door. I went as far as the lobby with them. Sellers put Calhoun in a police car where a local cop was waiting and they drove away. I went to the public phone in the lobby and called Bertha.

"I'm down here at Calexico," I said. "I'm still in Unit Seven at the Maple Leaf Motel. I'm probably going to be around here for a while. For your information, I just got some more money out of our client and instructions to go ahead . . ."

"Money out of our client!" Bertha yelled. "Where is he? And how the hell did you do that?"

"He's down here."

"How long's he going to stay?"

"Probably some little time," I said. "Frank Sellers and a local officer just arrested him for murder."

"Fry me for an oyster!" Bertha said.

"I'll take it from there," I told her, and hung up while she was still sputtering.

8

I found that Anton Newberry, with offices in El Centro, the county seat of Imperial County, had the reputation of being the best criminal lawyer in the county.

I didn't have any difficulty getting in to see him.

He took one of my business cards and said, "Cool and Lam, Private Investigators, eh?"

"That's right."

"And you're Donald Lam?"

"Right."

"What can I do for you, Mr. Lam?"

"I have a client in jail in Calexico. He'll probably be transferred to El Centro."

"What's he charged with?"

"Murder."

Newberry was a wiry, raw-hided individual in his late forties or early fifties, with high cheekbones, eyes spaced wide apart, a high forehead and a quick, nervous manner.

"When was he arrested?"

"About an hour ago."

"Who made the arrest?"

"A local officer accompanied by Sergeant Frank Sellers of the Los Angeles Police Department."

"What does Sellers have to do with it?"

"He was investigating the dope-running angle of the case. I think he's been working on it for a while.

"The victim is a dope runner named Eddie Sutton. He was killed last night or early this morning. The body was found in a houseboat on a trailer parked in Calexico."

"What's the name of our client?"

"Milton Carling Calhoun."

"Money?" he asked.

I took two hundred-dollar bills from my pocket. "This," I said, "is in the nature of a retainer. You're to see Calhoun and make arrangements for compensation with him, and you'd better be sure he gives you the true story. I think he'll try not to."

Newberry's long, thin fingers wrapped themselves around the money. "What's the story that he gave to you?" he asked.

I said, "The guy's evidently well fixed. He's married. It's been one of those cat-and-dog propositions. They're splitting up. Each one has an attorney. They're fighting over property."

"How much property?"

"Apparently a good deal."

Newberry folded and pocketed the two hundred dollars, then thoughtfully explored the angle of his jaw with thumb and forefinger. His face showed keen interest.

"Calhoun," I said, "is worried about publicity, particularly on a certain angle of the case."

Newberry twisted his lips in a wide grin.

"Funny?" I asked.

"Funny as hell," he said. "Los Angeles millionaire comes down to Calexico, gets himself arrested for murder. Los Angeles police are cooperating with the local authorities, and the guy would like to cut down on publicity.

"One thing I can guarantee," Newberry went on, "there'll be headlines all over the front page of the local paper tonight, and the story will be good enough to make the wire services. In all probability a feature writer for the Los Angeles papers will be down here by this time tomorrow looking for an interview."

Newberry picked up the telephone and said to his secretary, "Get me the chief of police at Calexico on the line—I'll hold on."

He sat there with the phone at his ear. I could hear the numbers click as his secretary worked the dial in the outer office.

Then Newberry said, "Hello, Chief, this is Anton Newberry, El Centro. . . . How's with you? . . . Good, eh? . . . You've got a client of mine down there by the name of Calhoun . . . How's that? . . . Oh, I see . . . Well, thanks a lot. I'll catch him up here."

He held on for a minute, then shook his head. "No comment," he said, "but thanks a lot for the information."

He hung up the telephone, turned to me and said, "The guy was brought up here an hour ago. He'll be in the jail here by this time. I'd better go over."

"Sounds like a good idea," I said.

"You're a professional licensed private detective?"

"Right."

"How much assistance from you can I count on?"

I said, "I'm going to investigate the case, but I'm going to do it my way."

"I'd like to have you work under me."

"Probably you would, but I've had experience in this game. I want to use it."

"I've had quite a bit of experience myself."

"Doubtless you have. Perhaps you'll have more before we get this case buttoned up."

"You've done some work so far?"

"Yes."

"Can you tell me about it?"

"Calhoun can tell you about it."

"But you'll keep in touch with me?"

"I'll keep in touch with you."

"And give me information as you get it?"

"I'll pass on the things I think you should know."

He thought that one over, then asked, "What evidence do they have against Calhoun?"

"I think Calhoun owned the murder weapon, a thirty-eight Smith and Wesson revolver.

"The dead guy came across the border last night, driving a Ford pickup with a pontoon houseboat on a trailer behind. The pontoons were cleverly made so that a cap could come off the ends and they could be stuffed with dried marijuana. They took quite a load.

"He got across the border all right, then parked the car by the side of the road. How's your coroner here?"

"Pretty good."

"You'll need a really good medical examiner, one who's a real expert in forensic medicine."

"Why?"

"I have an idea the time of death may be one of the most important bits of evidence in the whole case."

"How come?"

I said, "The evidence shows that Sutton had crossed the border by ten-fifteen at the latest. I think he picked a good parking place off the highway. He either had a scout car waiting there or one joined him there. The scout car went on ahead and found a roadblock. The driver radioed back for Sutton to wait it out. Sutton was tired. He got out of the pickup, went back to the trailer, climbed up, opened the door of the houseboat, and went in to take a rest.

"It's a small houseboat but, apparently, equipped with a gas stove for making coffee, a table, chairs, a bed and probably a water tank and some of the conveniences. While it's small, it looked pretty swank to me."

"You saw it?"

"I saw it."

"When?"

"When it came across the border."

"Did you see this man, Sutton, when he was driving the pickup?"

"I saw him when he was driving across the border and I saw him ten or fifteen minutes before that."

"Where?"

"In a restaurant in Mexicali."

Newberry looked at me thoughtfully. "You know," he said, "*you* could be involved in this case."

"Were you thinking of involving me?" I asked.

Newberry chose his words carefully. "I will be representing my client, Calhoun," he said, "and if it should appear— well, now, mind you, I'm saying that if it should appear from the evidence that there would be any chance of taking the heat off him by directing suspicion toward you, I won't hesitate for a split second."

"Thanks for telling me," I said.

Newberry had a habit of blinking his eyes rapidly when he was thinking, and from the way he was blinking I had an idea he was giving the situation a lot of thought.

"The more I think of it," he went on slowly, "you are in a rather vulnerable position. Where were *you* at the time of the murder?"

"Probably in Unit Seven at the Maple Leaf Motel in Calexico."

"How far from the scene of the murder?"

"Not far."

"And you saw the driver at a restaurant in Mexicali?"

"Yes."

"Talk with him?"

"No."

"Had you seen him before?"

"No."

"Did you know who he was?"

"No."

"When did you next see him?"

"When I was walking across the border. The Ford pickup
and the trailer with the houseboat on it were waiting in line
to get across."

"So you probably crossed the border just before he did?"

"Probably."

"Anybody who can back up your story?" he asked.

"I sleep alone," I told him.

Newberry shook his head. "It may be a most unfortunate
habit, Lam."

He pushed back his chair. "I'm going over and see my client.
Where can I reach you if I want you?"

"At the Maple Leaf Motel in Calexico, for the moment."

"Will you keep in touch with me as you move around?"

I shook my head. "There probably won't be time."

He said, "Why do you think the time element of the murder is so important?"

"Because Calhoun was just leaving Los Angeles at about the
time Sutton was crossing the border with the houseboat.
Sutton ran into some delay. His scout car hit a roadblock, so
Sutton went back to the houseboat to wait it out. If that

roadblock was on all night, that's one thing. If it was off before midnight, that's another thing. It may be important. If Sutton didn't go on after the roadblock was lifted, it could mean he was dead at that time."

Newberry asked, "What was the condition of the houseboat when the police discovered the body? Was there a light on or had the battery that furnishes juice for the lights been run down? Had the bed been slept in? Was there a dirty coffee cup? Was there—"

"The police," I said, "are singularly uncommunicative. They wanted to get Calhoun's story before they gave out any facts."

"They didn't get Calhoun's story?"

"No."

"Why not?"

"I advised him to see a lawyer before he talked," I said.

"Anything else?" Newberry asked.

I said, "Eddie Sutton had a companion with him when he crossed the border."

"Male, female?"

"Male."

"Description?"

"Can't give it. He was on the far side of the pickup and the light was such that I could only see the figure of a man."

"Do the police know that?"

"They know it."

"And they know that you saw this companion?"

"They know that."

"We would, of course, like to know who that companion was."

"We would all like to know who he was."

"Any ideas?"

"Nothing I can talk about."

Newberry was thoughtful. "You know, Lam," he said, "I think I can use you."

"One way or another," I said.

Again he grinned. "One way or another—no hard feelings if I try to pin this on you?"

"No hard feelings."

"And you'll let me know if you uncover anything that will help my client?"

"Probably."

"But you won't confer with me and cover the case under my directions?"

"No, I play a lone hand."

"All right," he said. "I'm going over to the jail and see my client."

He shook hands, a strong, sinewy hand that gripped mine hard.

"And you were in Calexico at the time the murder was committed?"

"Apparently."

"Good luck, Mr. Lam," he said. "You may need it."

He went out. I stopped at the desk in the outer office to get his secretary to give me one of his cards with telephone numbers on it; then I got in the agency car and drove back to Calexico.

9

I did a lot of thinking on the road back.

Nanncie had left the Maple Leaf during the early morning hours. She had gone either north or south. She wasn't apt to have gone either east or west. She had gone by taxicab or in a private car.

I had more legwork to do.

It didn't take me long to cover the taxicabs in Calexico. I drew a blank.

If Nanncie had gone south, she could have gone to San Felipe. Someone must have taken her in a private car. If she went north, she probably would have returned to Los Angeles by bus. But that wouldn't have been smart under the circumstances.

If Calhoun had been the one to call on her there at the motel, he couldn't have taken her very far. He had driven down from Los Angeles. He was tired. He might have taken her to the north as far as El Centro, or he might have taken her south—across the border.

I decided to check the really modern hotel in Mexicali as being the most logical place to look.

The Lucerna is an up-to-the-minute hotel with a patio, swimming pool, cocktail lounge and luxurious rooms.

I parked my car and walked out to stand by the pool, looking over the people who were basking in the Baja California sunlight.

I thought some of quizzing the hotel clerk as to whether some young woman had checked in early in the morning, but I thought better of that when I took stock of the situation.

The Mexican is an innate gentleman. If I had been able to get a Mexican police officer to go with me I could have secured the information; but to try to get it out of the clerk cold turkey was out of the question. The señorita's business would have been her own business and money wouldn't have changed the situation very much.

I was trying to think what Calhoun would have done—what he had done—what he had told Nanncie.

It had been some emergency which had caused her to check out and . . .

Suddenly I stiffened to attention. Nanncie, in a two-piece suit that showed a bare midriff, carrying a towel over her arm, came out and seated herself in one of the sunning chairs around the swimming pool.

I had a chance to take a good look at her. Then I went to where I had parked the car, unlocked the trunk, took out my baggage, and registered in the Lucerna Hotel.

Ten minutes later I was in my trunks and dunking in the pool. I came out, picked a chair which wasn't exactly the right style to suit me, got up, moved around and finally dropped into a vacant chair next to Nanncie.

I debated whether to make a pickup and get acquainted the slow way or whether to hit her right between the eyes.

99

I decided to hit her right between the eyes. There wasn't time for the slow way.

I looked straight ahead at the people in the swimming pool and said, "Nanncie, why did you check out of the Maple Leaf this morning?"

She jumped as though I had jabbed her with a needle, sucked in her breath as though to scream, then thought better of it and looked at me with wide, startled eyes.

I watched her out of the corner of my eyes but kept my face straight ahead.

"Who . . . who are you?"

"Donald Lam," I said, as though that explained everything.

"No, no, I don't mean your name. I mean who . . . how do you know who I am and what is it you want?"

I said, "I'm looking for Colburn Hale."

"What makes you look here and why ask me?"

"Because I'd like to have your help."

"Why do you want him?"

"I want to talk with him."

"About what?"

"Dope smuggling."

Again she caught her breath.

There was an interval of silence. "You're a detective?" she asked.

"Private," I said.

She thought for a few moments, then said, "I'm afraid I can't help you, Mr. Lam."

"I think you can. How did you get over here, Nanncie? You left the Maple Leaf Motel this morning, but you didn't have any car and you didn't come by taxi."

"A friend drove me over."

I made a shot in the dark. "You came here with a man who is driving a Cadillac automobile," I said.

"Lots of men drive Cadillac automobiles. If you must know, I'm hiding out."

"But you were waiting for Hale at the Monte Carlo Café last night."

She said, "He was supposed to meet me there right around seven o'clock. He said if he didn't show up within an hour I wasn't to wait but was to start protecting myself."

"Why did you check out of your apartment in Los Angeles, putting all your things in boxes and taking them to the storage company?"

"Because I'm in danger. We're both in danger."

"Meaning you and me?"

"No, meaning Colburn Hale and myself."

"On account of that dope information you gave him? The information you got from the hairdresser?"

"I'm afraid Cole is in trouble. He was to have met me last night and would have unless something terribly urgent had prevented him.

"He was to have followed that dope shipment up, getting the license number of the automobile and all that, and then he was to look me up. The dope runner was to go to the Monte Carlo Café to see if the coast was clear. He was to meet a confederate there, so Cole said I was to go there at seven and wait. While I was waiting I could look the situation over. After last night he'd have all the information he needed to file his story. He had some editor who was waiting for it."

"Now, let's get this straight," I said. "You picked up the tip originally in a beauty shop?"

"Yes, my hairdresser is very friendly and she was going with a man whom she didn't care too much about, but he was a good spender and she was playing along with him. Then suddenly she found out that he was smuggling dope across the border. She didn't know exactly how, but she had enough proof so that she didn't want any part of it. The guy was not only smuggling it across but he was pushing it, particularly with school kids."

"All right," I said, "she told Colburn Hale?"

"No, she told me. She didn't intend to tell me all the details but she let the cat out of the bag enough so that I could put Colburn Hale on the track of a beautiful article."

"What did he do?"

"He picked up the trail of the dope smuggler in Los Angeles."

"Eddie Sutton?" I asked.

"Uh-huh. How did you know?"

"I've been working on the case for a while myself."

"Well, he picked up Eddie's trail and followed him around, getting some surreptitious pictures of him near some of the high schools, and I think he even got a picture of a delivery being made. You know, one of those deliveries where they slip a person an envelope while they're brushing against each other casually and things like that."

"Then all of a sudden Colburn cleared out of his apartment and you cleared out of yours?"

"We got in trouble," she said.

"How come?"

"Hale was a little careless, a litt—well, I guess you'd say a little unskillful. The man he was tailing followed *him* and found out where he lived."

"Then what happened?"

"My beauty-shop operator hadn't broken off with the guy. She was still playing along with him, and he told her that some guy—he thought it was a hijacker—had moved in on him; that he was going to take care of the fellow, and he asked the operator if she knew me. So my friend knew that . . . well, anyway, I knew we were both in danger."

"So you told Hale?"

"I told Hale."

"Who else did you tell?"

"No one. We just both got out without leaving any back trail."

"But why come to the border?"

"Because Colburn Hale knew that this shipment was due to come across and he wanted to find out just how it came across. The smuggler was to pick up an accomplice—what they call a scout car—at the Monte Carlo Café. Cole Hale was to meet me there right after that had been done. I was to try to get a line on the accomplice and then Cole would join me."

"After they'd already found out about him, didn't he realize he was taking desperate chances?"

"He did, and he didn't. It would be risky, of course. But he thought he could follow the shipment up and find out just how it was coming across."

"That was a crazy thing to do," I said. "You're both a couple of rank amateurs and you're playing this like rank amateurs."

She said nothing.

"Now," I said, "Hale will be in trouble. Did the shipment come across last night?"

"I don't know, but I think it did."

"Why did you check out this morning?"

"I . . . I thought it was dangerous staying where I was there in the Maple Leaf."

"Who told you it was dangerous?"

"I . . . I just felt it."

"Try again," I told her.

"How's that?"

I said, "Try again and this time try to make it a little more convincing."

She flared up and said, "I don't have to account to you for everything."

"You don't have to," I told her, "but you'd better. Now, suppose you tell me about Milton Carling Calhoun."

"What about him?"

"Everything about him."

She said, "I'll tell you about that because I have nothing to conceal. Milt and I are good friends, and that's it."

"How good?"

"As friends, very good."

"You knew he was married?"

"Of course I knew he was married. Now, you listen to me. I don't like the tone of your voice and I don't like the look on your face.

"You've heard a lot about married men who string a girl along, telling her they're going to get divorced and when they're free they'll marry her and all that stuff.

"Nine times out of ten even if they *think* they're telling the truth, they aren't.

"The situation is different with Milton Calhoun. I met him at a sort of bohemian party. He was getting a kick out of talking with the people on the—well, on the other side of the tracks. He's very wealthy, you know."

"Is he?"

"I'll say he is."

"All right, so you met him at this party, and then what happened?"

"He and I sort of struck it off. He asked me if I'd go out to dinner with him some night during the week and I told him I would.

"So then he came out like a gentleman and told me that he was married, that he was having trouble with his wife, that they had separated, that he was living in a separate apartment, that he had moved out of the big house and left that to her, that there were no children, and that was that."

"And you've seen quite a bit of him since?"

"Quite a bit of him."

"And you're also friendly with Colburn Hale?"

"I am very friendly with Colburn Hale and I have half a dozen other men friends. I'm gregarious and I move around with a crowd that is gregarious. We like to live. We like to laugh—and I don't see where all this is any of your business."

I said, "We've got to do something about Colburn Hale. He was getting an article on this dope smuggling."

"That's right."

"And he told you he was going down to San Felipe and follow the shipment up?"

"Well, not in so many words, but I gathered that was what he was going to do. He told me to meet him last night at the Monte Carlo Café. He said he was due there around seven o'clock; that if he didn't show up right on time to wait for him for an hour."

"So you waited two hours?"

"Not quite two hours, but pretty close to it."

"Did it ever occur to you that he might be in danger?"

"Of course it occurred to me. Why do you suppose we checked out the way we did and didn't leave any back trail? We're dealing with people who are playing for keeps."

"Hale had his own car?"

"Yes."

"Anything distinctive about it?"

"No, it's just an ordinary black . . . Now, wait a minute, there is too. The left front fender has been struck and pushed up. He's been going to have it fixed but . . . Well, he's been busy and he hasn't had too much money."

"You don't have a car?"

"I don't have a car."

"All right, how did you get from the Maple Leaf Motel down here?"

"Milt drove me across."

"You mean Milton Calhoun?"

"Yes."

"And how did he find you?"

"I don't know. He came to the window and called my name about . . . I don't know, it was along in the night. He asked me to open the door so he could talk with me."

"And you did?"

"I opened the door and I was a little bit annoyed. I told him that I didn't appreciate being called in the middle of the night that way and that he didn't have any claims on me and that I was annoyed.

"Then he told me to keep my voice down, to get my things packed up; that I was in danger and he was going to move me to some other hotel. He finally convinced me and I packed up and got in the car with him and he drove me across here, registered, and paid for the room for three days in advance."

"What are you going to do at the end of that three days?"

"I don't know, but I presume that by that time the story will have broken and there'll be no further danger from those dope smugglers."

"You sound to me like a bunch of amateurs trying to climb a perpendicular rock face," I said. "You just don't know what you're getting into. You're dealing with professionals."

"What would you suggest doing?" she asked.

"The first thing we'd better do is to try to find Colburn Hale. He's evidently somewhere between here and San Felipe. Get your clothes on and we'll take a ride."

She said, "I think he can take care of himself all right. He . . . he had a gun."

"What kind of a gun?"

"A thirty-eight-caliber revolver."

"Where did he get the gun?"

"I gave it to him."

"And where did you get it?"

"I got it from Milton."

"Now, wait a minute," I said. "Let's get this straight. Milton Calhoun gave you a thirty-eight-caliber gun?"

"That's right."

"When?"

"A couple of days ago when he first learned that I was working with Cole on a deal involving some dope smuggling. He told me that I could get in a lot of trouble that way and that he wanted me to be protected."

"So he gave you the gun?"

"Yes."

"His gun?"

"Of course it was his gun, if he gave it to me."

"And then you gave that gun to Colburn Hale?"

"That's right."

I did a lot of thinking. Then I said, "Come on, we're going to drive down the road to San Felipe and keep our eyes open on the side roads."

"Why?"

"Because," I told her, "we may find a car with a front right fender that's been bent up and a dead body in it."

"A dead body!"

"Your friend, Colburn Hale."

"But he . . . they . . . they wouldn't dare . . ."

I said, "You're dealing with a professional bunch of dope smugglers. Their deals run into the thousands of dollars. A murder now and then is more or less of an incident. Get your clothes on and meet me here in as close to five minutes as you can make it."

She hesitated for a moment, then got to her feet and said, "Well, perhaps that's the best way, after all."

10

The road from Mexicali to San Felipe runs for some distance through a territory where there are occasional roadside restaurants selling ice-cold beer to the thirsty traveler together with a few of the more simple Mexican dishes.

There are some houses along this section of road before it crosses a barren stretch of desert to climb through a mountain pass. The Gulf of California is on the left, the barren desert on the right, and to the south the heat-twisted volcanic mountains where the hot desert winds have blown the sand high up on the rocky slopes.

I had settled for a long run and we had gone some distance in silence. Then Nanncie said to me, "I don't want you to get me wrong. I don't play my boyfriends one against the other. I am gregarious. I'm fond of people. I'm a writer. I don't want to give up my career so I can be a housewife and raise squalling babies. I'm not cut out for that kind of work. I'm ambitious."

"You're living your own life," I told her.

"And," she went on, "I want you to know that I didn't have anything to do with breaking up Milt's home. He and his wife had separated before I ever met him, and I never did furnish a shoulder for him to cry on about how she didn't understand him or how cold she was . . . But I will admit I gave him a taste of the sort of life he had never seen. A taste of bohemian life, a taste of associating with people who were living by making their minds work. A rather precarious living, I'll admit. But that's not because of any lack of talent on the part of the people who are doing the writing. It's on account of editorial policies."

"What's wrong with editorial policies?" I asked.

"Everything," she said. "The good magazines have a tendency to close the doors against free-lance writers. They have more and more adopted a policy of staff-written contributions.

"And then the bigger magazines cater to the big names, the people who are well established."

"And how do you get to be well established in the literary world?" I asked.

"By having your stuff published."

"And how do you get your stuff published?"

She smiled and said, "By getting to be a big name. You can't . . . Donald! Donald, there's Cole's car!"

"Where?"

"Over at that roadhouse restaurant parked right by the open-air kitchen. See that fender?"

I swung my car off the road and we came to a stop by a somewhat battered old-model car that was parked against the rail of an open-air dining room.

There was no one in this dining room, but I opened a door which led to a rather cramped interior and suddenly Nanncie was flying past me with outstretched arms. "Cole! Oh, Cole, oh my God, how glad I am to see you! Tell me, are you all right?"

The man who had been sitting at the table drinking beer got stiffly to his feet.

He and Nanncie embraced, completely oblivious of me.

"I made it," he told Nanncie, "but it was touch and go."

"Cole, you've got a black eye and there's blood on your shirt!"

"And my ribs are sore and I've taken a beating," he said.

She remembered me then. "Cole, I want you to meet Donald Lam. Donald, this is Colburn Hale."

Hale backed away suspiciously, ignoring my outstretched hand. "Who's Lam?" he asked.

"A detective," she said. "A . . ."

Hale started to turn his back.

"A private detective," she said. "A private detective who has been looking for you."

Hale turned back. He regarded me with suspicious eyes, one of which was badly swollen and had turned purple, the eye being bloodshot underneath the discoloration.

"All right," Hale said, "start talking."

I said, "I know just about everything there is to know. When Nanncie told me that you were going to meet her at the Monte Carlo Café at seven o'clock last night and didn't turn up and when I knew that the shipment of dope you had been tailing had crossed the border, I thought it might be a good idea for us to drive down the road toward San Felipe and see if we could find some trace of you."

"Well, you waited long enough," Hale complained.

"There were other matters claiming attention," I told him. "Why don't we go outside where we can talk? Bring your beer along and perhaps you can give me some information and perhaps I can give you some information."

"Perhaps," Hale said, but he picked up the bottle and glass of beer and carried them along with him.

He was a suspicious individual. He didn't wear a hat and had a shock of wavy, dark hair. I estimated him at about a hundred and eighty pounds, about five foot eleven or so.

The guy had surely been in trouble. In addition to his black eye he had evidently had a bloody nose and some of the blood was still on his shirt.

He hadn't shaved for a couple of days and his skin had that oily look which comes from extreme fatigue.

We sat down at a table in the outdoor dining room. There was no one else in the place. I ordered a couple of bottles of ice-cold beer.

"You seem to have had a beating," I told Hale.

He said, ruefully, "I thought I was smart, but I was dealing with people who were smarter than I was."

"Who gave you the beating?"

"Puggy."

"Who's Puggy?"

"Hell, I don't know his last name. All they called him was Puggy."

"And how did Puggy happen to meet you?"

"I was following a dope shipment."

"We know all about that," I said.

"No, you don't," he said. "Nanncie may have told you what she knows, but she doesn't know all the details. The—"

"She does now," I said. "The little houseboat on pontoons that makes regular trips up and down from San Felipe on a trailer drawn by a Ford pickup. The pontoons are made with a removable cap on the rear, so cunningly fitted that it looks like a welded job. But the cap slides off and the interior of the pontoon is filled with dried marijuana."

"And how do *you* know all this? Hale asked.

"The authorities know it now," I said.

"The hell they do! Then my story has gone out the window."

"Perhaps not," I said. "There are other angles which may make your story newsworthy, provided it's dramatic enough."

"Well, it's dramatic enough," he said.

"What happened?"

He said, "Nanncie got wind of what was happening. She tipped me off to the dope smuggling and the people who were doing it, but I needed to have some firsthand information. I couldn't do it all on hearsay. I had to know just how the stuff came across.

"Anyhow, I got pretty much of the first part of the story together and was typing it like mad when Nanncie got in touch with me late at night and told me we had to run for cover fast."

"Why?"

"The beauty operator who had told her had let the cat out of the bag and Nanncie was in danger, and if she was in danger, I would be, too. They had followed me when I was tailing them."

"So what did you do?"

"I didn't want to have a bunch of dope runners on my trail. These men are desperate. I decided to move and not leave any back trail. I also decided to bust that gang of dope runners and not disclose my identity until after they had been captured and were serving a term in prison.

"So I packed up everything in my apartment. I got a friend of mine to help me and we moved out, stored my stuff, and I drove to Mexicali where I knew that these dope runners made their rendezvous."

"Go on," I said.

"I knew who was doing the dope running and I knew they were smuggling it in at Càlexico, but I didn't know all of the details and I wanted to get a story based on firsthand observation.

"Anyhow, I picked up this dope runner, a man they called Eddie. If he's got another name I don't know what it is. He was driving a Ford pickup. I thought at first the stuff came up in that pickup, but I followed him down to San Felipe and saw that he hitched onto a houseboat that was mounted on a trailer, a small houseboat on pontoons.

"I knew that the shipment was due to cross the border at seven o'clock last night. I knew that much because I heard Eddie talking about the second car that was to pick him up at Calexico."

"The second car?" I asked.

"The second car," he said, "equipped with Citizen's Band radio. That's the way they work. After the stuff gets across the border at Calexico, they send a scout car on ahead. The scout car is absolutely clean. Anybody could search it all day and couldn't find even a cigarette stub that had any pot in it.

"That car goes on ahead, quite a ways ahead. If there's a roadblock of any kind, or if the border patrol has a station where they watch the road, this scout car sends a message back to the car with the dope by Citizen's Band radio. So then the dope car turns off or may turn clean around and go back.

"You understand, Lam, I'm telling you this in confidence. I want the exclusive story rights to it. You also understand that we're dealing with something big here. This isn't any little two-bit dope-smuggling outfit that brings in a few pounds at a time. This is big stuff. They're dealing with many thousands of dollars."

"Go ahead," I told him.

"Well," Hale said, "I knew that the scout car with the Citizen's Band radio was to be waiting just north of the border so that it could pick up the dope car, but I didn't know it was being followed by a muscle car that was to come along behind. I suppose I should have. I guess I was dumb."

"What happened?"

"I started trailing that Ford pickup with the houseboat on the trailer from San Felipe. I didn't have any trouble until we got almost up here, then suddenly the muscle car closed in on me."

"What happened?"

"Some fellow wanted to know who I was following and who the hell I thought I was. He was abusive and the first thing I knew he'd slugged me."

"What did you do?"

"I slugged him back, and that was the mistake of my life. This guy was evidently an ex-pugilist. I think that's where he got the name of Puggy. The driver of the car called him Puggy, anyway."

"And what did they do?"

"I took a shellacking," Hale said, "and then I had a gun and I made up my mind I wasn't going to take any more. I jumped back and pulled the gun, and that's where I made my second mistake. I found myself looking down the barrel of a sawed-off shotgun that the driver of the pickup had produced out of nowhere."

"So what?"

"So," Hale said, "they took my gun away from me. They put me back in my own car which Puggy proceeded to drive. They went down a side road which they knew and they tied me up good and tight, stuck a gag in my face, and warned me that the next time I wouldn't get off with just a beating. In fact, the driver of the car wanted to kill me, but Puggy said the Mexican drug ring didn't like murders and they wouldn't commit one unless they had to."

"Go on," I said.

"I stayed trussed up in that confounded car all night," Hale said. "Then this morning about eight o'clock a fellow driving along the side road from some ranch saw the car parked there, stopped to look it over, and found me, bound and gagged in the rear of the car. By that time my circulation had stopped. I was as stiff as a poker and so sore from the beating I'd taken I could hardly move."

"Keep talking," I said.

"Well, he was shocked, of course, but he untied the ropes and . . ."

"Untied them?"

"That's right."

"Go ahead."

"He untied the ropes and took the gag out of my mouth, put me in his car, took me to a ranch house, and he and his wife gave me hot coffee, then some kind of a Mexican dish of chile and meat, some tortillas, and the native kind of white cheese and some sort of fish.

"They were awfully nice people."

"How far from here?" I asked.

"Oh, ten, fifteen miles, something like that. I don't know exactly. Right down where a side road turns off and goes around the head of the Gulf."

"Can you find the place again?"

"I guess I could, yes."

"You'd better find it," I said.

"Why? And who the hell are you to be quizzing me like this?"

"I'm doing it," I told him, "because you're going to have to collect all the evidence you can get."

"Why?"

"Puggy took your gun away from you?"

"Yes."

"And where did you get that gun?"

115

He hesitated and looked at Nanncie.

Nanncie nodded her head. He said, "Nanncie gave it to me."

"Where did Nanncie get it?" I asked.

He shook his head. "She didn't tell me. She said she had it for her protection and she thought I needed it more than she did."

I said, "For your information, Eddie, whose last name was Sutton, accompanied by another man who was probably Puggy, crossed the border with the load of marijuana about ten o'clock last night. It had started to rain and they were two hours late—and I guess the fact that Puggy had to take care of you threw them off schedule a bit.

"Anyway, Sutton pulled off to the side of the road to wait for the scout car to go ahead and report a clear road. He and Puggy evidently got in some kind of an argument over the division of the profits or perhaps over the fact that they hadn't killed you to silence you and—"

"Wait a minute, wait a minute," Hale said. "I'll bet they sent a car back to finish the job."

"What makes you think so?"

"After I'd been lying in that car what seemed like ages another car came down the road and seemed to be looking for something. It came down the road and went back two or three times."

"You were close to the road?"

"I was close enough to the road so I could be seen by daylight, but a man coming down on a dark night, trying to find me by the headlights on a car, could very well have missed the car . . . I'll bet that was what it was all about. I'll bet they came back to take care of me, probably to drive me out someplace where they could load me aboard a boat, take me out in the Gulf and throw me overboard with weights tied

116

to my neck and feet. It had started to rain. The night was as dark as pitch and the guys couldn't find me.

"I was desperate at the time. I tried to make noises to attract the attention of the driver. I realize now it's one hell of a good thing that I didn't."

"All right," I said, "that's probably true."

"What happened after that?" he asked. "You said Puggy and Eddie got in a fight about something?"

"Puggy and Eddie got in a fight about something," I said. "I imagine that Puggy started putting pressure to bear on Eddie about the fact that you needed to be taken care of on a permanent basis. Anyway, they got in a fight and Eddie got killed."

"Got killed?" Hale said.

"Got killed," I said.

"How?" Hale asked.

"One shot from a thirty-eight revolver," I said, "and I wouldn't be at all surprised if the revolver that fired the fatal shot wasn't the gun Puggy had taken away from you, the one that Nanncie had given you so you could protect yourself, and the same gun that had been given Nanncie so that she could protect herself."

Hale looked from me to Nanncie, then from Nanncie to me, then back to Nanncie. "Did Milt give it to you?" he asked Nanncie.

She nodded her head.

Hale reached an instant decision. "Don't tell anybody about where you got that gun," he said. "Let Calhoun explain it. He's got plenty of money, plenty of pull, and he'll get the best lawyers in the country. Don't let them drag you into it. Let's let Calhoun shift for himself."

117

11

I paid for the beers at the outdoor restaurant and said to Hale, "Come on, you've got to pilot us down to the place where you spent the night. What happened with the ropes they tied you up with?"

"They're in the back of my car."

"Did you get the names of the people?"

"José Chapalla," he said.

"They talk English?"

"Oh, yes."

I walked over to look at the ropes in his car. They were a heavy fishing twine. When a knot is tied in this stuff it can become very tight indeed.

I picked up the ropes and looked at the ends.

"What are you looking for?" Hale asked.

I said, "It's a shame your Mexican friend didn't know more about police science."

"What do you mean?"

"A good police officer," I said, "never unties a rope that

a person has been tied up with. He cuts the rope and leaves the knots intact."

"Why?"

"Sometimes you can tell a good deal about a person from the type of knot he ties."

"Oh, you mean a sailor and all that stuff."

"A sailor, a packer—and sometimes just a rank amateur. Come on, let's go. You'd better get your car and we'll follow you. How far is it?"

"I would say around ten miles. But let me go with you, if you will, so I can stretch out. Nanncie can drive my car. I've had a real beating and I'm sore. My muscles are sore, my ribs are sore."

"I know," I told him. "I can sympathize with you. I've had several beatings."

He climbed slowly, laboriously into the back of the car. "Gosh," he said, "I'd love to have some hot water and a shave and get cleaned up."

"In a short time you will," I told him. "This is going to be my party from now on. I'm going to take you to the Lucerna Hotel in Mexicali. You can get a good hot bath and crawl into bed. Then you can get out in the swimming pool and float around and gradually exercise those muscles until you get the stiffness out of them."

"That sounds good," he said. "Boy, I'd sure love to get in a warm swimming pool and just relax and take all the weight off of myself and just float."

"It can be done," I told him.

We drove down to La Puerta where the road turns off to the east to go around the head of the Gulf.

"This is the road," Hale said.

We drove down the road for some distance; then Hale said, "This is where they left the car."

I got out and looked around.

119

I could see tracks where a car had been driven off the road, then where it had been standing perhaps a hundred yards from the edge of the road. There were footprints all around where the car had stood, lots of footprints.

We went back to the road and drove on . . .

"That's the place," Hale said, "that adobe house over there."

It was an unpretentious adobe house with an old dilapidated pickup in front of it.

I stopped the car and got out to knock on the door. Nanncie pulled up behind us and parked.

Hale eased his way out of the car and shouted, "Oh, José —Maria. It's me. I'm back."

The door opened.

A Mexican, somewhere in his fifties, with a stubby black mustache and a shock of black hair, attired in overalls and a shirt that was open at the throat, stood in the doorway, smiling cordially.

Just behind him, peering over his shoulder, I could see the intense black eyes of the man's wife.

"Amigo, amigo!" he called. "Come in, come in!"

Hale hobbled along and introduced us. "José and Maria Chapalla," he said. "They are my friends. And these two are my friends, Miss Nanncie and . . . What did you say your name was?"

"Lam," I told him.

"Mr. Lam," he said to the Mexicans.

"Please to come in," the Mexican said.

We entered the house, a place which had been designed to shut out much of the powerful sunlight, a place that was comfortable with the smell of cooking.

There was a fireplace with bricks built up so that a big iron pot could rest between the bricks. Underneath this iron pot was a small bed of coals, and by the fireplace were some sticks with which to keep the fire going.

To the left of the fireplace was an oil-burning stove with a battered tin coffeepot and a covered cooking pot in which a Mexican dish was simmering slowly, the cover lifting from time to time to let out a little spurt of steam.

The aroma of rich cooking filled the place.

Hale said, "My friend here wants to know about how you found me. Can you tell him the story?"

Chapalla said, "Sit down, sit down," and then became embarrassed as he realized there weren't enough chairs for all of us.

"Please to be seated," he said. "I prefer to stand when I tell the story."

We seated ourselves.

His wife, Maria, a heavily built Mexican woman with a chunky frame and a smile of good-natured hospitality, busied herself at the stove.

"Would you perhaps have coffee?" Chapalla asked.

"We haven't time," I said. "We're fighting against minutes. If you could just tell us how you found the car, it would be of great help."

"It is *muy mala*," Chapalla said. "Bandits have hurt this man very bad and left him tied up."

"How did you find him?"

"I am going to get some food," he said. "Our trips to the store are not many. When we go we take the pickup and we get much stuff.

"I am driving. I see this car off the road. At first I think nothing of it. I drive by it.

"Then I say to myself, 'José, why should that car go over there and be left. If there is trouble with the motor the car would be on the road. If it is driven over there, what is there to make the driver go to that part of the country to stop his car?'

"I drive on.

"But I think. I think. I do more thinking. Then I stop, I back up, I turn around. I go over to the car. At first I see nothing. Then I look inside. I see something that is light. It is the cloth that has been tied in your friend's mouth.

"I say, '*Caramba*, what is this?' I try the door of the car. It is not lock. I open it. Your friend is inside. He has been tied with a fishing cord in which knots are very tight indeed."

"You turned him loose?"

"I turned him loose."

"Did you cut the cords?"

"No, I am afraid. The cords are tied too tight. Maybe a slip of my knife and there is blood."

"Did you have a hard time untying the knots?"

"Not too hard. My fingers are very strong, señor. I have been a fisherman. I work much with lines. I know knots."

"And you took out the gag?"

"The gag?"

"The cloth in the mouth," I said.

"Oh *seguro*, sure. I take out the cloth and he speaks to me, but after some difficulty."

"What does he say?"

"He says he has been held up."

"And then?"

"So then the man is suffering. I invite him to come to my house."

"Does he drive his car?"

"No. He goes with me. He cannot get in the driver's seat of his car because he is sore in the sides of the stomach and his nose has bled and his eye is black.

"He has had a beating, that one!"

"And then what?" I asked.

"So we came to my *casa* and Maria she makes the hot food —tortillas, some *chile verde* that we have cooking, some *frijoles refritos*, some cheese . . . He eats much, this man. He is sore, but he is hungry."

"And then?"

"Then we have him lie down on that bed. He lies still and he sleeps. Then he gets up and he leaves. I drive to his car."

"How long ago?"

José shrugged his shoulders. "I do not have the watch— maybe one hour, maybe two hours."

"And that is all you know?"

"That is all I know."

I nodded to Hale, "All right," I said, "we're going to Mexicali and I'm putting you in a good hotel. I'll bring you a sports shirt and . . . Where's your razor?"

"In my bag in the back of the car. It was in the back of the car. My God, do you suppose they took it?"

"Let's look."

He got the car keys and unlocked the trunk. A big bulging bag was in there, together with a smaller suitcase.

"Everything okay?" I asked.

"Apparently so," he said with relief. "You won't need to get me a new shirt. I have clean clothes in my bags, thank heavens."

"All right," I told him, "let's go."

"But there is a matter of money," Hale said. "I am a writer and . . . I had gambled much on this story and . . ."

"Pay it no mind," I told him. "The party is on me from here on."

The expression of relief struggling with his black eye was ludicrous.

Maria continued to busy herself over the stove, smiling a farewell and saying simply, "Adios."

I handed her a ten-dollar bill. "I make my thanks to you for the help you have given," I said.

They didn't want to take it, but it was apparent the money meant much to them. Maria finally took it with fervent thanks.

José Chapalla came to the door. He shook hands with all three of us. "*Vaya con Dios*—go with God," he said.

12

We stopped at a service station where there was a hose with running water. Hale washed the most noticeable bloodstains off his shirt and washed his face.

Nanncie tooted the horn of Hale's car and waved as she passed us on her way to the hotel.

Hale was doing some thinking en route.

When we stopped he said abruptly, "You're working for Milton Calhoun?"

"I'm working for him."

"I'm not," Hale said. "To be perfectly frank, I don't like the bastard."

"I'm working for him," I repeated.

"And," Hale said, "I'm not going to go out of my way to give him any help. He's got money, he can hire lawyers and . . ."

"He's already hired a lawyer. I want you to talk with him."

"I don't know whether I'll talk or not," Hale said.

"Suit yourself," I told him, "only don't forget one thing."

"What's that?"

"I'm working for Calhoun."

"Okay by me," he said. "You can work for anybody you damn please."

We entered the hotel. I escorted Hale to the desk.

The clerk smiled and shook his head, put his hands on the counter palms up. "I am so sorry, señors, but there are no vacancies. We are full and . . ."

"He is a friend of mine," I explained. "He has been in an automobile accident."

The clerk became all smiles. "Oh, in that case, *seguro*, yes, but certainly, we will take care of him."

He pushed a pen and a card in front of Hale and Hale registered. I noticed that he gave his address as 817 Billinger Street.

I saw that he was fixed comfortably in his room, got the bellboy to bring in his big bag and suitcase from his car and said, "You don't want these ropes that you were tied up with any more, do you?"

"I never want to see them again," he said.

"I'll get rid of them for you," I told him.

I took the ropes and put them in the trunk of the agency heap, drove across to Calexico, telephoned the office of Anton Newberry and asked the secretary if Newberry was in.

"He's just leaving for the day," she said.

"This is Donald Lam," I said. "Tell him to wait until I get there. I've got news for him."

"What kind of news?"

"It may be good news."

I could hear the mumble of off-the-telephone conversation; then the secretary said, "He'll wait. Try to get here as soon as possible."

"It won't be long," I told her. "I'm already across the line."

I made time to El Centro, was fortunate to find a parking place, and climbed the stairs to Newberry's office.

The secretary ushered me to the inner office where New-berry was waiting for me.

He twisted his thin lips in a smile which lacked cordiality.

"I hope it's good news, Lam," he said, "and it must be important."

"It is."

"Just what is it?"

"Sit down and get your notebook," I said. "You'll want to take notes."

"I have a tape recorder and I can put you on tape."

"I'd prefer to tell you the story and have you make notes."

"Why?" he asked.

"For various reasons."

"All right," he said, "tell me why you think it's good news."

I said, "It's about the gun that did the fatal shooting."

"Tut, tut, we don't know what gun did the fatal shooting."

"But the police have found it—a thirty-eight-caliber revolver that's registered to Milton Carling Calhoun."

"How do you know it is the murder weapon?"

"I'll bet ten to one."

"I never bet against a client. They haven't done the ballistics work yet, and . . . I believe they have traced the registration. The gun was purchased some time ago by Mr. Calhoun, but that isn't necessarily conclusive."

I said, "I can account for the gun."

"Without involving Calhoun?"

"Without involving Calhoun."

His face lit up. This time the smile was cordial. "Well, well, well," he said, "tell me how it happened."

I said, "Calhoun gave the gun to a girl."

He shook his head and said, "We can't have any of this, Lam. We can't have any women brought into the case. Not at all, do you understand that?"

"I understand it. You are the one who decides what's going

to be brought into the case. I'm the one who gives you the facts so that you know what to keep out of the case."

He nodded his head emphatically. "Very smart of you, Lam," he said, "very smart. Now, tell me about the gun."

"The girl," I said, "gave the gun to a fellow by the name of Colburn Hale. He's a writer. He was working on a story dealing with dope smuggling and—"

"Yes, yes," Newberry interrupted, "I've talked with my client. I know all about Hale."

I said, "No, you don't."

"What don't I know?"

"Lots of things. That's what I'm here to tell you."

"Go ahead."

"Hale," I said, "was given the gun for his protection. He went down to San Felipe and started playing around with this bunch of dope runners. I don't know when they made him, but probably about as soon as he left San Felipe on the trail of the shipment.

"They let him get as far as the vicinity of La Puerta; then the tail car closed in on him."

"The tail car?" he asked.

"There were two cars," I said. "The dope was in the lead car, a Ford pickup. It had Citizen's Band radio communication. The man who was driving it could communicate with the car behind."

"Why the tail car?" Newberry asked.

"The muscle car," I said.

"I see."

"In the vicinity of La Puerta, they used the Citizen's Band radio to instruct the muscle car to close in."

"And what happened?"

"The muscle car closed in. They worked Hale over pretty well and then Hale made the mistake of pulling his gun. He's very lucky that he isn't dead today. But down there in Mexico the people who run the drug shipments don't like to have murders. Drug shipments can be explained as a matter of course, but a corpse is something else again and the Mexican authorities don't like it.

"The Mexican dope rings want to be as inconspicuous as possible."

"Go ahead."

"So the dope shipment came to a stop and the guys moved in on Hale.

"Hale got beaten up in the process. Then they tied him up and left him in his own car."

"What about the gun?" Newberry asked.

"They took his gun. The point is, it wasn't his gun. It was Calhoun's gun, one that he had given his girl friend for her protection, and the girl friend, thinking Hale was in the greater danger, had passed the gun on to him.

"Now, that's the story. You can take it or leave it."

"Where's Hale now?"

"I've got him stashed."

"You found him when he was tied up?"

"I found him after he had been untied and set loose. A Mexican rancher by the name of Chapalla found the car with Hale in it and untied the ropes."

"What kind of ropes?"

"A fishing cord—heavy fishing cord."

"Then there must have been at least three men in the dope ring," Newberry said thoughtfully.

"Not necessarily. Sutton could have been driving the dope car. A man named Puggy could have been the one driving the muscle car. They left the muscle car south of the border and Puggy could have got in with Sutton when they came across. Puggy could have been the man I saw sitting beside Sutton in the pickup."

"And then there was a man driving a scout car," Newberry said.

I shook my head. "Puggy was probably the one to drive the scout car. They left the muscle car parked south of the border; then they came across and went to the point where they had a third car stashed, and Puggy was to take that and drive ahead and make sure the coast was all clear. So Puggy came to a roadblock and radioed back to Sutton that he'd better lie low for a while."

"There was a roadblock near Brawley last night. The Highway Patrol was checking cars from about eight o'clock until midnight," Newberry said.

"That explains why Eddie Sutton waited in Calexico," I told him. "He was waiting for the coast to clear. Puggy found the roadblock, radioed the alarm, and then drove back to join Eddie. They had an argument. Eddie got shot."

"It sounds very nice," Newberry said, and then added, "the way you tell it. However, there are certain facts which are very significant."

"Such as what?"

"Such as the fact that you were the one who found the fatal gun. You said it had been thrown in a field. No one saw it thrown it the field. You could have carried the fatal gun across with you and dropped it. You could have been intending to go away and leave it there until someone found it, but a sharp-eyed, ten-year-old kid followed you over and wrecked your plan.

"You're a private detective. You are pretty smart. You were tailing a dope shipment that was worth many thousands of dollars and a dope ring that was worth a lot more money. You could very easily have decided to cut yourself in for a piece of cake. Sutton wouldn't go for it.

"I don't think you'd kill Sutton in cold blood like that,

but if you had this gun you might very well have beaten Sutton to the punch."

"And where would I have got the gun?" I asked.

"That," Newberry said, "is something my client insists is not to be brought out no matter what the provocation. That's your ace in the hole. It gives you a chance to beat the rap if anyone moves in on you."

"And I have a good lawyer, of course."

"And you have a good lawyer, of course," he said, smiling.

"You've had a talk with your client?" I asked.

"I've had a very comprehensive and satisfactory talk with him. I think I know more of the case than you do—unless, of course, you did the killing.

"Now then, my technique is to have a preliminary hearing just as soon as possible. I don't intend to call any witnesses or put on any defense. I want to get that over with fast. I want them to bind my client over for trial in the Superior Court. Once we get to the Superior Court, we'll really tear this case upside down.

"However, I am going to subpoena you as a witness at the preliminary because I may want your testimony perpetuated before you change it. I may tip the prosecutor off to you as a witness."

He grinned.

Newberry opened a drawer and whipped out a subpoena which he handed to me. "The preliminary hearing starts tomorrow morning at ten o'clock," he said. "This is your subpoena to be there."

"What about Colburn Hale? Do you want him there?"

Newberry said, "I don't care about Colburn Hale tomorrow. I'm going to use that boy in the Superior Court hearing. Have you seen the El Centro papers?"

"No, why?"

He walked over to a table, picked up a newspaper, and handed it to me. There were screaming headlines across the front page.

LOS ANGELES MILLIONAIRE JAILED FOR MURDER HERE—and then in smaller headlines, ATTORNEY NEWBERRY INSTRUCTS CLIENT TO SAY NOTHING.

I read the newspaper account. There wasn't much in it, but what they had had been stretched way, way out. A sergeant of the Los Angeles Police Force, on the track of a big dope ring, had flown to Calexico and joined forces with the police there. The shipment had been brought across in the pontoons of a small houseboat on a trailer. The body of Edward Sutton, presumably a dope smuggler, had been found in the houseboat. He had been shot with a .38-caliber revolver.

Police had later found that .38-caliber revolver where the murderer had sought to dispose of it by throwing it into an alfalfa field some little distance from the scene of the crime.·

While I was reading the article, Newberry was busy looking at my face, blinking his eyes all the while.

All of a sudden he said, "This Colburn Hale, he's positive that he had the gun the night of the shooting and they took it away from him?"

"That's right."

"And there was another man named Puggy who was in on the deal?"

"Right."

"And you saw two men in the pickup when it crossed the border?"

"Correct."

Newberry's face broke into a slow grin. "On the other hand," he said, "I think I'll make a grandstand. I may want this man, Hale, in court so I can get a statement. Can you get him to come to court?"

"Give me a subpoena for him and I'll try."

"What's the name?" he asked.

"Colburn Hale."

"It won't do any good to serve this subpoena across the line," Newberry said.

I grinned at him and said, "Do you suppose Hale knows that?"

Newberry matched my grin. "Not unless somebody tells him," he said.

"All right," I told him, "give me the subpoena. If you want him there, I'll try to have him there. He is not very pretty. He's got a beautiful shiner, and . . ."

"Wonderful, wonderful!" Newberry said. "Certainly we want him there. We want his picture in the paper—a mysterious witness who will clear my client in the Superior Court. We can let the newspapers get the story—pictures—black eye —wonderful!"

"There is one thing *I've* got to have," I said, "if I'm going to get Hale in court."

"What?"

"The opportunity to see Calhoun—now."

He shook his head. "It's too late. Visiting hours are . . ."

I pointed to the telephone. "You can fix it up," I said.

"It might be a little difficult."

I said, "Calhoun is paying you to smooth out difficulties."

He picked up the telephone, put through a call to the Sheriff's Office, talked a while in a low voice, hung up the phone, turned to me and nodded.

"It's all fixed," he said. "You'll have to go right away."

"On my way," I told him.

He was watching me speculatively as I left the office.

13

Milton Calhoun had the best quarters in the Detention Ward. I don't know whether money had fixed it or whether Anton Newberry had pull, but the place wasn't too bad as jails go.

He was glad to see me.

"How do you like the attorney I got for you?" I asked.

"I think he's all right," he said.

"He's arranged for a quick preliminary hearing," I said, "tomorrow morning at ten o'clock, I understand."

Calhoun nodded and said, "But the preliminary hearing means nothing. We're not going to do anything except ride with the punch. That's what Newberry thinks should be done."

I said, "Have you talked to anybody?"

"Newberry, that's all."

I said, "Sit tight. Don't talk to anybody. Don't give anyone even the time of day. Refer them to Newberry."

"That's what my attorney has told me."

"All right," I said. "Now I'm going to tell you a few things. Get over closer."

"Why closer?" he asked.

"So you can hear me better," I said.

I sat on one side of the toilet and motioned Calhoun to the other side.

I flushed the toilet, put my lips close to his ear, and started talking about Colburn Hale.

When the toilet ceased to make noise, I quit talking, waited for a few seconds, then flushed it and began all over again.

"What's that for?" Calhoun asked.

"That," I said, "is because the place is bugged and I don't want other people to hear what we're talking about. Why didn't you tell me that you knew where Nanncie was?"

"I didn't want anyone to know."

"You act like a clumsy fool," I said. "You can't hold out information on me any more than you can on your lawyer."

"I haven't even told him all you know," Calhoun said.

"Then don't. I'm going to take care of Nanncie. Be sure that you don't ever mention her name. They'll ask you about the gun and . . ."

A man appeared at the barred door. "What the hell is all this water running down the toilet about?" he asked.

I grinned at him and said, "How did you know water was running down the toilet?"

He looked at where Calhoun and I were seated on opposite sides of the toilet, shook his head, and said, "Come on, wise guy. Get out. Your visit is over."

"That was a short visit," I said.

"Wasn't it?" he agreed.

"Why cut it so short?" I asked.

"Because," he told me, "we don't like to waste water. We're out here in the desert. Come on, let's go."

I shook hands with Calhoun. "Remember what I told you," I said.

I followed the deputy sheriff on out.

The deputy had me check out on the visitors' register, looked me over and said, "Sergeant Sellers told us about you."

"Do you," I asked, "want *me* to tell *you* about Sergeant Sellers?"

He had the grace to grin. "That won't be necessary," he said.

After I got out of the jail I bought the El Centro evening paper. Seated in the agency car, I read about Calhoun. Evidently he was a real big shot in Los Angeles.

Then another item caught my eye.

Headlines read: ROADBLOCK NEAR BRAWLEY NETS MANY CARS WITH DEFECTIVE EQUIPMENT.

I read about the forty-two cars with defective lights, and then I read: "Peter L. Leland, a former pugilist, was also apprehended at the roadblock at 10:45 P.M. An alert officer spotted Leland waiting on the outskirts of the roadblock, communicating over a Citizen's Band radio with some unkown individual. Inquiries developed that Leland was wanted, having jumped bail in Los Angeles on a charge of dope smuggling. He was taken into custody."

I tore this out of the newspaper and put the item in my billfold. This could be Hale's "Puggy." I debated whether to call the matter to Newberry's attention, but decided to wait until I saw him at the preliminary hearing.

I drove across to the Lucerna Hotel and found Colburn Hale sitting fully clothed by the side of the swimming pool, talking with Nanncie. Nanncie was in a bathing suit.

"What's the matter?" I asked Hale. "No swim?"

He shook his head. "Just too plain sore to even think of it."

"It'll take the soreness out of you. Relaxing in water is one of the best ways there is to get your muscles unwound."

"I suppose so," he said, "but it's—it's just a problem even getting my clothes on and off. I managed a hot bath. I almost fainted. I'll wait a couple of days before I swim."

I said, "I have a little missive for you."

"What is it?"

I handed him the subpoena.

"Why, that's tomorrow morning at ten o'clock!" he said.

"That's right."

"In El Centro."

"That's right."

"Well, I suppose if I have to be there, I'll have to be there."

I said, "I've got one just like it."

"What about me?" Nanncie asked.

I shook my head and said, "You don't have anything to contribute to the situation at the present time, at least nothing that anyone knows about.

"And," I went on, looking pointedly at Hale, "*I know that no one will say anything that would drag your name into it.*

"It's getting late. I'll buy you folks a drink."

Hale eased himself up out of the chair.

"I'll shower and dress," Nanncie said. "It'll take me a few minutes."

"You can join us in the cocktail lounge," I said.

Hale started staggering and hobbling toward the cocktail lounge. I said, "Oh, just a minute, I forgot something."

I went back to where Nanncie was just getting up.

"Get your things all packed," I said. "You've got to get out of here."

"Why?"

"To keep your name out of the papers."

"But how am I going?"

"I'm taking you."

"Where am I going?"

"To a place where no one will ever think to look for you. Say nothing to anyone. Join us in the lounge for a drink, then make an excuse to get to your room. I'll give you a buzz."

I rejoined Hale. We went into the cocktail lounge and had a

Margarita, one of those beautiful Mexican drinks with frosted salt around the edge of the glass and a cool balm of liquid delight inside.

Nanncie joined us. We had another drink.

Hale would have sat there and pinned one on, but I said I had some work to do and left.

Nanncie said she never cared for more than one drink before dinner, and we left Hale sitting there.

Things worked out like clockwork. Nanncie was packed all in one suitcase and a bulging bag. She had made a record for speed.

I tipped a bellboy, and while Hale was still in the bar we were were on our way.

"Where," Nanncie asked, "are we going?"

I said, "You are going to go to a primitive place."

"Where?"

"Ever hear of El Golfo de Santa Clara?" I asked.

She shook her head.

"This," I said, "is a place down on the Gulf on the Sonora side. It's clean, it's nice, it's quaint, it's picturesque. There's a motel there that is fairly livable, and there are some very good restaurants where you can get perfectly fresh seafood and prawns that are almost as big as a small lobster.

"There's only one thing you'll have to put up with."

"What's that?"

"The water in the shower," I said, "is at what they call room temperature."

"And what is room temperature?"

"Pretty damn cold if you take it in the morning," I said.

"How long do I have to stay there?"

"Until I come and get you."

"Can't you telephone the . . ."

I shook my head. "I told you," I said, "I was taking you to a place that's isolated. No reporter is going to find you

138

there. No one is going to find you there, not even Sergeant Frank Sellers of the Los Angeles Police Force, who is probably going to be looking for you."

We started out. We had a long, long drive ahead of us, but if they found her at El Golfo de Santa Clara, they could get rich finding needles in haystacks.

14

Even taking a shortcut by way of Puertecitos and Riito, it's a long ways from Mexicali to El Golfo de Santa Clara, but one thing was certain—no one was going to be looking for a missing witness at El Golfo.

From the time the road passes Riito, it runs down as a straight and virtually deserted ribbon through barren desert country until it comes to the place where it drops down from the higher country and comes to the alluvial deposit of the Colorado River near the Gulf.

Then, after a few miles, one comes to El Golfo de Santa Clara, a little fishing village, beautifully picturesque, where a fishing fleet is tended by an ancient amphibious "duck" which goes from boat to boat as a sort of water taxi, bringing in fish and passengers.

The fish are used to supply the local restaurants and are the overflow of the cargoes which the fishing fleet keep iced for commercial deliveries.

Here also is where the supply of clams for the California

markets comes from. Miles and miles and miles of tideflats are literally filled with clams. Clammers take light boats with outboard motors, drive them up over the mud flats, wait until the tide goes out, then start gathering clams. By the time the tide comes back in high enough to float the boat, the clammers will have a load of clams which, when brought to the United States, will command a fancy price.

Aside from that and the few tourists who know of the fishing and the clamming, El Golfo basks serene and deserted in the sunlight of the Gulf.

The motel there is clean with indoor plumbing and showers in the Mexican style which tend to flood the floor of the bathroom whenever a shower is taken, and the water, as I had remarked, was at "room temperature."

Nanncie was a good sport and I felt she could put up with things and be happy.

On the way down I had a chance to get acquainted with her.

"You must think I'm something of a tramp," she said.

"Why?"

"Well, I have done so much for Cole Hale and I'm friendly with Milt Calhoun and I'm—I have quite a few friends."

I could see she wanted to talk so I just devoted my attention to driving the car.

She said, "It's hard for an outsider to understand the way we live—us writers."

Again I kept quiet.

She said, "It's sort of a society of its own, a freemasonry. We have very close friendships, but we're not prepossessed with sex the way some people think. It's more like an organization where everybody is just a close friend, as though we were all men or all women. We have so many things to think of, so much to do, so much to keep us occupied.

"Life is something of a struggle. We have to support ourselves and it's a grim fight, but it's a lot of fun.

"We watch the mail for envelopes, rejection slips with the returned manuscripts, and now and then a check.

"For the most part, we hit the smaller markets, the religious magazines, the trade magazines. We sell fillers, little articles, sometimes a short story of fiction.

"We all seem to keep just about one jump ahead of the landlord, and after you get to be a real part of the gang you can make a touch once in a while if a person has sold two or three good articles in succession and you're up against it for the rent. You can make a small touch to tide yourself over. But woe to you if you don't pay back at the first opportunity you have. The deadbeat is completely ostracized.

"It's hard to tell you how we work out there on Billinger Street. It's something like—well, from all I can hear, it's like Greenwich Village in New York used to be many, many years ago."

"And Milton Calhoun fits into that picture?" I asked.

"He emphatically does not fit into that picture," she said, "and that's why I'm afraid of him. Milt wants to be received as a friend, but you know instinctively that he isn't one of us. If I married him I'd be jerked out of the environment I love so well. We'd be on the French Riviera, or cruising in yachts. If I wanted to have my friends visit me in that environment I'd be uncomfortable and so would they.

"Right now Milt tries hard to be one of the gang, but despite the act he puts on he's an outsider."

"Do you mean he's a hypocrite?" I asked.

"No, no, no, I'm afraid you don't know what I mean. You don't understand what I'm trying to tell you.

"Milt thinks that is a poor life. He would like to rescue me from that life. That's the way he thinks of it, as a rescue. He would like to marry me when he becomes free and give me a big house and servants and a yacht and all the stuff that still goes with extreme wealth."

"And you don't want it?"

"I don't want any part of it, not the way I feel now. I like Milt. I'm tremendously fond of him. I could probably fall in love with him if I'd let myself, but I love this life that I'm living, this being just one jump ahead of the landlord, this studying the magazines, the writer's magazines, looking for tips on what can be sold and where it can be sold.

"Sometimes I'm a little behind in the rent, sometimes I've even been short on postage, but I'm one of the gang. We all of us sort of pull together. It's a great life and I like it."

"Perhaps," I said, "you're getting the cart before the horse."

"What do you mean?"

"Perhaps you ought to rescue Calhoun."

"Rescue him from what?"

"From the same thing he's trying to rescue you from."

"I don't get it."

"From the life he leads," I said.

"Oh," she said, then laughed. "He'd like that!"

"Here's a guy with money running out of his ears. He puts in his day turning to the financial column of the papers, reading the stock listings, giving orders to his brokers, having all the accessories of wealth including a dissatisfied wife. You could save him from all that."

"Yes," she said, laughing. "I've even thought of that. Suppose I did marry him and had all the glittering embellishments of wealth. Pretty quick he'd be burying his nose in the financial page at breakfast and then hurrying away to give orders to his brokers. I'd be sitting there—I won't say a bird in a gilded cage because it's too damn much of a cliché, but you know what I mean."

"I know what you mean," I said.

"Why not tell Calhoun that if he'll cut himself off from his bank account and move down on Billinger Street, take up writing and support himself by his earnings, you'll feel different about it?"

She laughed gleefully. "It would be a great gag at that. I'd like to see his face when I pull that on him."

"And Hale?" I asked. "What about Hale?"

"Hale," she said, "is one of the gang. He's a friend.

"Good Lord, I run onto a chance to give him a real first-class article on dope smuggling. It's something that a man has to do —a woman can't do it.

"So I pass the tip on to Cole Hale and do everything I can to make the story jell."

"And what will you get out of it?"

"It depends upon what Cole gets out of it. He'll cut me in for a percentage."

"And you'll take it?"

She looked at me in surprise. "Sure, I'll take it," she said. "What do you think I'm doing this for?"

"I thought perhaps it was from a sense of devotion."

"Don't be silly," she said. "I like Cole, but I have a living to make just as he has a living to make."

"So you're in this thing together?"

She nodded.

"And in deep," I said.

Again she nodded.

After a while she said, "You're the one I don't get. I don't get the sketch."

I said, "I'm a private detective. I have loyalty to the person who employs me. I don't have all of the immunities that an attorney would have. As a result I have to protect myself and my client.

"For instance, I can't hold out evidence on the police if the police demand that evidence, and I can't conceal evidence that would tend to solve a case on which the police are working. If I did I'd be in trouble."

"But you're concealing me."

"No, I'm not," I told her. "I'm just taking you where you're not going to be disturbed by a lot of newspaper reporters."

"Newspaper reporters?"

"That's right. Have you seen the evening papers?"

"No, I guess I haven't."

"Well," I said, "the evening papers are making a big feature of the Los Angeles millionaire who was arrested for murder."

"But he hasn't said anything about me, has he?"

"He hasn't said anything about you, but don't underestimate the skill of the reporters."

"But how could the reporters find anything that would lead to me from the fact that Milt Calhoun has been arrested?"

"They'll talk with Calhoun's attorney," I said. "His attorney will be very mysterious. He won't mention any names, but the name of Colburn Hale will be brought into the case. Then the reporters will start talking with Hale."

"Do you think he will talk?" she asked.

"Do you think he'll keep quiet?" I countered.

She thought that one over and said, "Then why don't you spirit him away?"

"Because," I told her, "Hale is a witness. He enters into the case. The police wouldn't like it if a private detective spirited Hale away. And don't get the idea that I'm spiriting you away. I'm just taking you to a place where you won't be disturbed and where you can get a good rest."

"All right, we'll let it go at that," she said, laughing.

We let it go at that.

By the time we got to El Golfo I felt that I knew Nanncie very well indeed and she was one nice kid. I could see her viewpoint. I didn't know how long she'd have it. I knew that sooner or later some guy would sweep her off her feet and I knew that it might well be Milton Carling Calhoun once he learned the proper approach, but I didn't think it was my duty as his private detective to give him the proper approach. It was up to him to find that out for himself.

We got into El Golfo in time to get two rooms in the motel. I told Nanncie, "There's a bus service out of here that you can take if you have to, but you won't be hearing from me, you won't be hearing from anybody, unless someone comes to get you."

"And suppose someone comes to get me?"

"Then," I told her, "you'll have a nice long ride."

"Will we have breakfast together in the—"

"I'll be long gone by breakfast," I told her. "I have work to do."

I filled up the agency heap and took Nanncie over to the little restaurant café. It was late, but they still had some fried prawns and I saw the surprise on her face at the quality of the food.

"Just watch that you don't get fat," I warned.

"What am I going to do for money?" she asked.

"How much do you have?"

"Damn little."

I laughed and said, "You have no objection taking money from me which came from Milton Calhoun as expense money?"

"Get this straight, Donald. I have no hesitancy whatever in accepting money from you for anything."

I handed her a hundred dollars.

She looked at the money with wide-eyed surprise.

"This," I said, "is going to have to last you for a while. Don't try to account for it. Just put it in as a hundred dollars' expense money, and if you have any left when you get home, just forget about it."

"But this is your money."

"There's more where that came from."

She hesitated, then folded the money and put it in her purse. I had an idea it was more money than she'd had at one time in quite a spell.

We finished our dinner. I got her a couple of bottles of Tehuacán mineral water and a bottle opener to keep in the room, told her it was better to drink Tehuacán, the mineral water of Mexico, than it was to take a chance on drinking tap water.

When I started to say good night, she reached up and kissed me.

"Donald," she said, "I don't know whether anyone has ever told you, but you're a very wonderful person."

"Are you telling me now?" I asked.

She said, "I'm telling you now," and kissed me again.

15

I was up before daylight and on the long, lonely road north, leaving the tideflats behind me, climbing up into the higher desert, then driving for mile after mile.

The east lightened into a glorious orange, then into blue, and the sun burst over the mountains to throw long shadows from the greasewood and the desert plants.

Finally I came to the turnoff.

By this time it was broad daylight.

It was a job getting to El Centro in time for the preliminary hearing, but I made it.

The deputy district attorney was a man named Roberts, Clinton Roberts, and he took himself rather seriously.

He started out by making a speech to Judge Polk who was holding the preliminary hearing.

"The purpose of this hearing, if the Court please, is not to prove the defendant guilty of a crime, but simply to show that a crime has been committed and that there is reasonable ground to believe the defendant is connected with the commission of that crime."

Judge Polk frowned slightly as though he objected to being educated by a much younger man.

"This Court understands fully the scope of a preliminary hearing, Mr. Prosecutor," he said. "You don't need to explain it."

"I am not explaining it, if the Court please," Roberts said. "I am trying to set forth the position of this office. Because of the prominence and social standing of the defendant we are going to go further than would ordinarily be the case. We are going to introduce enough evidence to show fully what the prosecution will rely on at the time of trial. And if the defendant can explain that evidence we will be only too glad to have such explanation made so that the case can be dismissed at this time."

Anton Newberry, twisting his thin lips into a grin, said, "In other words, you are inviting the defense to show its hand at this preliminary hearing?"

"Not at all," Roberts said angrily. "We are simply trying to show that the prosecution will conduct its case according to the highest standard of professional ethics and that if the defense can explain the evidence we will be only too glad to join with the defense in asking the Court for a dismissal."

"And if the defense makes no explanation?" Newberry asked.

"Under those circumstances," Roberts snapped, "we will ask that the defendant be bound for trial in the Superior Court on a charge of first-degree murder."

"Go ahead with your evidence," Judge Polk said to Roberts.

Roberts called the county surveyor to the stand to introduce the diagram he had made showing a section of the road between Calexico and Imperial.

There were no questions on cross-examination.

Roberts introduced the testimony of a Calexico police officer who was on patrol duty on the night of the nineteenth and the morning of the twentieth. He had noticed the pickup with the houseboat trailer parked at a wide space in the road very near the northern boundary of the city limits of Calexico. He had seen it earlier in the evening of the nineteenth and he saw it shortly after midnight on the morning of the twentieth. He decided to leave the occupant of the houseboat alone until morning and then waken him to tell him that there were laws against camping there by the roadside and that, while he didn't want to be arbitrary, he would have to insist that the occupant move on.

The officer had knocked on the door repeatedly. There was no answer, so he tried the handle of the door. The door was unlocked. He opened the door and looked inside and saw a body sprawled upon the floor.

He came to the conclusion that the man had been shot. He immediately backed away and closed the door, being careful as he closed the door not to leave any more fingerprints.

He had then radioed headquarters and they had sent out a team of investigators and had notified the sheriff in El Centro, who had sent deputies.

The officers had moved the pickup and houseboat to police headquarters at Calexico where there were facilities for a scientific investigation.

An expert fingerprint man from the Sheriff's Office had taken over and, within a short time, Sergeant Frank Sellers, an expert in homicide from the Los Angeles Police, who was frequently engaged in liaison work in outlying communities, had joined forces with the other officers.

Newberry said shortly, "No questions on cross-examination."

An officer identified on the diagram, which had already

been introduced, the place where the pickup and trailer had been located just within the city limits.

Again there was no cross-examination.

A Sheriff's Office fingerprint expert was called to the stand. He testified to painstakingly powdering the inside as well as the outside of the pickup and houseboat, searching for fingerprints.

Had he found any?

Indeed he had. He had found many latents that were smudged. He had found some seventy-five latents that couldn't be identified and he had found some latents that could be identified.

"The latents that could be identified," Roberts asked, "where did you find them?"

"I found five prints of a left hand that had been placed against the aluminum side of the houseboat just to the left of the door handle. One of the fingerprints, presumably the thumb print, was smudged. The other four latents were identifiable."

"Do you have photographs of the fingerprints?"

"I do."

"Will you produce those photographs, please?"

The witness produced the photographs.

"Now then, you say that those were identifiable. Have you identified those four fingerprints that were clear and unsmudged?"

"I have."

"Whose fingerprints are they?"

"The fingerprints of Milton Carling Calhoun, the defendant in this case."

There was a startled gasp from the spectators, and Newberry's eyes were blinking several times to the second, but his face was a wooden poker face.

Calhoun was the one who showed emotion. He looked incredulous and then chagrined.

This time Newberry made a perfunctory cross-examination.

"You don't know when those fingerprints were made," he said.

"No, sir, I do not. All I know is that they were made at some time before I was called on to go over the houseboat for fingerprints, and that was on the morning of the twentieth."

Was the expert absolutely certain these were the fingerprints of the defendant?

"Absolutely."

"Each print? Or was it the cumulative effect of the several prints?"

"No, sir," the expert said. He had identified each and every fingerprint. There had been enough points of similarity in each fingerprint to make an identification positive.

Newberry let the guy go.

A medical examiner summoned by the Sheriff's Office testified that he had journeyed with the county coroner to Calexico; that the body had been observed in place on the floor of the houseboat; that then the body had been removed to the mortuary and there had been a post-mortem. Death had been caused by a .38-caliber bullet which had penetrated the chest, severed a part of the heart, and lodged near the spine on the right-hand side of the body, traversing the chest at an angle. The bullet had been recovered. Death had been at some time between 9 o'clock at night on the nineteenth and 3 o'clock in the morning on the twentieth.

Newberry's cross-examination was perfunctory.

How had the time of death been established? The answer was that the witness had used body temperature and the development of rigor mortis and of post-mortem lividity, had taken into consideration the outer temperature that night, estimated the temperature inside the houseboat, etc.

"What about the stomach contents?" Newberry asked. "Had not the contents of the stomach given a definite idea as to how long after the last meal had been ingested before death occurred?

"The stomach contents would be of no help," the physician said. "The last meal had been ingested quite a few hours prior to death."

I passed a note to Newberry. "Find out about conditions in the houseboat," I said. "Was an electric light on at the time the body was discovered? Was there a gas stove which had been used and which would have changed the temperature in the houseboat and thereby thrown off the calculation of the time of death? And ask if it isn't a fact that rigor mortis develops sometimes very slowly and at times almost immediately, particularly if death occurs during the height of an argument or quarrel which has raised the blood pressure."

Newberry read the note thoughtfully, crumpled it, tossed it into the wastebasket, and said to the witness, "No further questions on cross-examination."

The witness left the stand.

The prosecution introduced a certified copy of the State Firearms Records showing that Milton Carling Calhoun had purchased a certain Smith & Wesson .38-caliber revolver with a one-and-seven-eighths-inch barrel, number 133347, the cylinder of which held only five shells. The weapon had been purchased from the Sierra Sporting Company in March three years earlier.

A photostatic copy of the record was introduced, showing the signature of Milton C. Calhoun and his address.*

* For the purposes of evidence a certified copy of the firearms register is introduced, but for the purpose of identifying the signature of Calhoun it re-

Roberts said, "I am going to call Sergeant Frank Sellers, of the Los Angeles Police, to the stand."

Sellers took the oath with the bored manner of one who had testified thousands of times.

The prosecutor asked questions showing Sellers' professional qualifications and the fact that he was in Calexico on the morning of the twentieth.

"What brought you to Calexico?" Roberts asked.

"Our department was asked by the chief of police of Calexico to furnish some technical assistance in connection with a matter—"

"Just a minute," Newberry interrupted. "Unless that matter is connected with the present case, I object to it as incompetent, irrelevant and immaterial."

"It is indirectly connected," Roberts said, "but we will withdraw the question."

Newberry smiled as though he had actually accomplished something besides keeping me from getting some information I would have liked to have had.

"But you were in Calexico on the morning of the twentieth?"

"Yes, sir."

"At what time in the morning?"

"I arrived by plane about five-thirty in the morning."

"And what did you do?"

"I reported to the police."

"And then what?"

"Then later on I went to the De Anza Hotel for breakfast."

"And what happened when you arrived in the De Anza Hotel?"

---

quires a photostatic copy of the original record. A certified copy only shows the contents of the original certificate. To show the signature on the certificate a photostat is required. E.S.G.

"I found a private detective, one Donald Lam, whom I had known and with whom I had had dealings on several occasions, and he was then and there accompanied by one Milton Carling Calhoun, the defendant in this case."

"Did you have any conversation with them?"

"Oh, yes. I asked Lam what he was doing there and was given to understand that he was working on a case and that the defendant in this case was his client."

"Then what?"

"Then a Calexico police officer came and asked me to join him for a few minutes and told me that a murder had just been discovered on the outskirts of town."

"I accompanied this officer to the scene of the crime, a houseboat mounted on pontoons and being in turn mounted on a trailer behind a Ford pickup."

"Did you search the premises for a possible murder weapon?" Roberts asked.

"We did," Sergeant Sellers said.

"Was any weapon found?"

"Not at that time."

"What do you mean by that?"

"I mean that the murder weapon was found at a later time."

"By whom?"

"I believe," Sellers said, "the murder weapon was discovered by Donald Lam."

"Is Donald Lam in court?"

"Yes, he is. He's seated there in the front row."

"I ask permission to withdraw this witness temporarily and to call Donald Lam to the stand."

"For what purpose?" Newberry asked.

"For the purpose of showing the finding of the murder weapon."

"I don't think that is proper procedure," Newberry said.

Judge Polk shook his head impatiently. "We aren't going to try this case on technicalities, not at this time and in this court. The witness will stand down while Donald Lam is sworn. Stand up, Mr. Lam."

I stood up.

"Hold up your right hand."

I held up my right hand.

The clerk said, "You solemnly swear that all of the evidence you will give in this case now pending before this court will be the truth, the whole truth, and nothing but the truth, so help you God?"

"I do," I said.

They asked me for my name, address and occupation, and I gave that information for the court records and seated myself in the witness chair.

Roberts, who had evidently carefully rehearsed the questions and was following a well-thought-out campaign, said, "You went out to the scene of the murder?"

"I don't know," I said.

"What do you mean, you don't know?"

"There was no corpse there when I got there."

"But you went to the place where the pickup and trailer had been located?"

"I don't know."

"Well, you went to what you thought was the place?"

"Objected to," Newberry said. "What the witness thought doesn't make any difference."

"All right," Roberts snapped, "I'll withdraw the question. I call your attention to this map or diagram of the northern portion of the city of Calexico, Mr. Lam. Does that mean anything to you? Can you orient yourself on that map?"

"Generally."

"I call your attention to certain marks here which represent the place where the witnesses have said the pickup and trailer with the houseboat were parked. Did you go to that locality?"

"I did."

"When?"

"I don't know the exact time. It was during the morning of the twentieth."

"Did you look for a murder weapon?" Roberts asked.

"I looked around. I wanted to see what evidence had been overlooked," I said.

Sergeant Sellers had the grace to wince. The deputy sheriff, who was sitting in court, frowned.

"And what did you do?"

"I looked around a place where quite a few people were present and then I walked over to the extreme edge of a wide place by the side of the road."

"Can you show us on the diagram, People's Exhibit A, where you walked?"

I went over to the diagram and indicated the place marked "Drainage Ditch."

"I walked along the edge of this drainage ditch," I said.

"What were you looking for?"

"Any evidence that had been overlooked."

"You said that before."

"You asked me; I tried to tell you."

"And what evidence did you think might have been overlooked?"

"I wanted to see if anyone had taken the trouble to cross that muddy ditch and look in the alfalfa field on the other side."

"Did you find any footprints indicating anyone had crossed the ditch?"

"I did not."

"Therefore, you felt that no one had crossed that drainage ditch since the water had left a deposit of mud in the bottom?"

"That's right."

"And what caused *you* to cross that ditch?"

"The fact that nobody else had."

"If the murderer had not crossed the ditch, what led you to believe that there was evidence which might have been found on the other side?"

"A man who throws a baseball doesn't necessarily walk to home plate," I said.

Someone in the audience snickered.

Roberts cleared his throat authoritatively. "You don't need to be facetious, Mr. Lam."

"I wasn't being facetious. I was pointing out a physical fact."

"In any event, you decided to cross that ditch?"

"I not only decided to, I did."

"And what did you do when you crossed the ditch? By the way, how did you cross that ditch?"

"I walked."

"No, no. I mean, what did you do about your shoes and socks?"

"I took them off and carried them."

"And you crossed the ditch and climbed barefoot up the bank on the other side?"

"That's right."

"Then what did you do?"

"I walked up and down the bank."

"And what did you find, if anything?"

"When I had arrived at a certain place which I will try to indicate on the map, I saw something metallic gleaming in the field. I moved over far enough to find that it was a revolver."

"And what did you do?"

"I told a young boy, who had followed me across, to call the police."

"Was that the first time you had seen this gun?"

"Yes, sir."

"Now, let's not have any misunderstanding about this," Roberts said. "I am showing you a thirty-eight-caliber revolver with a one-and-seven-eighths-inch barrel being numbered one-thirty-three-three-four-seven, and having five shots, or the places for five cartridges in the cylinder. Will you look at this gun, please, referring, if the Court please for the sake of the record, to People's Exhibit B?"

I looked at the gun and said, "This looks very much like the gun. I never did pick it up. I simply asked the young man to notify the police and to ask them to come at once. That is, I actually asked him to go to his parents and ask his parents to notify the police."

"Now, this young man, would you know him if you saw him again?"

"Yes, sir."

"Stand up, please, Lorenzo."

The ten-year-old kid, looking very bug-eyed, stood up in court.

"Is that the person?" Roberts asked.

"That's the person."

"You may sit down," Roberts said to Lorenzo.

Roberts looked at me long and hard, "Mr. Lam," he said, "I suggest that you had that murder weapon in your possession when you went out to the place which has been indicated on the map."

"I did not!"

"I further suggest that you looked around to find where would be a good place to conceal the weapon. That when you saw no one had crossed the muddy bottom of that ditch, you

159

decided that it would be a good plan to drop that weapon in the alfalfa field."

"I did not!"

"I suggest that you, therefore, went out into the alfalfa field; that you dropped the weapon; that you then intended to return to the bank on the other side and say nothing about what you had done, but that the presence of this young man, Lorenzo Gonzales, forced you to change your plan; that the keen eyes of this young man detected that you had something you were trying to conceal, and he asked you what it was, or words to that effect."

"That is not so."

"That because this young man was standing where he could, within a short time, and would undoubtedly have discovered this gun and, under the circumstances, the fact that you had planted the gun would have been immediately apparent, you changed your plans and pretended to have discovered the gun yourself and asked young Lorenzo to run to his parents and get them to notify the police."

"That is not true."

"I further suggest that you did this in order to protect your client, Milton Carling Calhoun."

"That is definitely not true."

"But you did very fortuitously discover this gun?"

"Yes."

"And by some stroke of reasoning, or perhaps I should say some stroke of genius, you were able to walk directly to the place where this gun had been dropped."

"That is not true."

"Why did you go there?"

"I was making a general survey of the terrain."

"And that survey caused you to take off your shoes and socks and wade across a very mushy, muddy ditch bottom in order to go to an alfalfa field where your keen mind suggested to you that the murderer might have been able to have thrown the gun without leaving any tracks in the bottom of the ditch?"

"I wanted to survey the territory. I crossed the ditch. I found the gun."

"And you had never in your life seen this gun before?"

"Oh, Your Honor," Newberry said, "I should have objected a long time ago, but I have let this farce go on because I thought perhaps counsel had some definite objective in view.

"I object to this entire line of questioning on the ground that counsel is attempting to cross-examine his own witness."

"The objection is sustained," Judge Polk said.

"And I now move to strike out the entire testimony of this witness on the ground that the testimony was improperly elicited and as the result of improper questions which were the result of an attempt to cross-examine the prosecution's own witness."

"The motion is denied," Judge Polk ruled.

Roberts said, "You wish to cross-examine this witness before I dismiss him from the stand and recall Sergeant Frank Sellers?"

"Certainly not," Newberry said. "I have no questions of this witness. Here is a man who came out to the scene of the crime and made an investigation which should have been made by the Sheriff's Office of this county and the police of the city of Calexico, to say nothing of the really great expert imported from Los Angeles."

And Newberry made a sarcastic bow in the direction of Sergeant Sellers.

Sergeant Sellers angrily half arose from his chair, but thought better of it.

"There's no need for any grandstand oratory at this time," Judge Polk pronounced. "You may stand down, Mr. Lam. And Sergeant Sellers will return to the stand."

"Now that we have the background of this murder weapon clarified somewhat," Roberts said, "will you please tell what happened as far as you know—of your own knowledge?"

"I was at the Calexico Police Station, talking with the Chief," Sellers said. "There was a phone call and I was advised by the Chief . . ."

"Just a minute, just a minute," Newberry said. "I object on the ground that any conversation that you had with the chief of police which was not in the hearing of this defendant is hearsay and incompetent, irrelevant, and immaterial."

"Sustained," Polk said somewhat wearily.

"Just tell us what you did following this conversation," Roberts said.

Sellers said, "I called to one of the police officers and asked him to drive me out to the scene of the crime."

"Was a deputy sheriff there at the time?"

"There were several deputy sheriffs at police headquarters, but they were working on developing latent fingerprints and doing other things. As a matter of fact, I didn't think much of this hurried tip . . ."

"Move to strike out everything after the words 'As a matter of fact.' " Newberry said.

Judge Polk said, "It may go out. Sergeant, you know that you are not to offer any opinion."

"I'm sorry," Sellers said. "That just slipped out. I was thinking of my reactions at the time and what I did, and how it happened that we didn't call any of the Sheriff's Office to go out with us."

"That's quite all right. That can come out in cross-examination, if at all," Judge Polk said. "Just go ahead with what you personally did and what you personally found, Sergeant."

Sellers, who was not enjoying himself in the least, shifted his position uncomfortably and said, "Together with this

Calexico officer I went out to the scene of the crime. This young boy, Lorenzo Gonzales, was there waiting for us. He said something to us which, of course, I can't repeat because it was not in the presence of the defendant, but, as a result of what he said, this officer and I walked across the ditch to a point where Donald Lam was standing over—that is, almost over, that gun, which as it turns out, is the gun marked People's Exhibit B and introduced in evidence in this case."

"And what did you do?"

"I inserted a fountain pen in the barrel of the gun so as to keep any fingerprints which might be on the weapon from being smudged. I elevated the fountain pen, thereby picking up the gun, and using this means of holding the gun in a perpendicular position, I carried it back across the ditch.

"We then took the gun to police headquarters where fingerprint men dusted it to try to develop latent prints.

"There were no prints on the gun. I may state that we hardly expected to develop latent prints on metal of this sort."

"There were no prints at all?"

"Objected to as hearsay," Newberry said.

Sellers grinned at him and said, "I was present when the dusting was done, Counsel."

"And there were no fingerprints?" Roberts asked.

"There were some smudges, but nothing that was identifiable on the gun."

"What was subsequently done with this weapon?" Roberts asked.

"I took it to the Office of the Sheriff in this county where a ballistics expert and I fired test bullets from it and put them in a comparison microscope with the fatal bullet in this case."

"And what did you find?"

"We found a perfect match."

"Meaning what?"

"Meaning that this weapon, which has been introduced in

evidence as People's Exhibit B, was the murder weapon, the weapon which fired the fatal bullet."

"I believe that I have no more questions at the present time of this witness," Roberts said. "You may cross-examine, Counsel."

Newberry thought for a moment, then said, "I have no cross-examination at this time."

"Call Lorenzo Gonzales to the stand," Roberts said.

Lorenzo, looking suddenly badly frightened, came forward.

"How old are you, young man?" Judge Polk asked.

"Ten—going on to eleven."

"Do you understand the nature of an oath?"

"Yes, sir."

"What does it mean?"

"It means that you have to tell the truth."

"And what happens if you don't tell the truth?"

"You are punished."

"And you are afraid of punishment?"

"Everybody is afraid of punishment."

"Administer the oath," Judge Polk said to the clerk.

The clerk administered the oath.

Roberts said, "You are acquainted with Donald Lam, the witness who testified here a short time ago?"

"Yes, sir."

"And what was he doing when you first saw him?"

"He was walking around the place where all the people were standing."

"And then what did you see him do?"

"I saw him take off his shoes and socks and cross over the muddy bottom of the drainage ditch."

"How were you dressed at the time?"

"I had on my pants and a shirt."

"The pants were long pants?"

"No, sir, they were the kind of an overall pants that had been cut off a little below the knee."

"And what about your shoes and socks?"

"I don't have none. I never wear shoes—except at church and—like when I come in here. Shoes hurt my feet."

"So you were barefooted at the time?"

"Yes, sir."

"So it meant nothing to you to run across the drainage ditch?"

"No, sir."

"Now, what caused you to cross the drainage ditch?"

Lorenzo, who evidently had been carefully coached, said, "I saw that this detective man had found something."

"Now, just a minute, just a minute," Newberry interrupted. "That question calls for a conclusion of the witness and the answer is a conclusion of the witness."

Judge Polk was interested. He leaned forward. "The Court will ask a few questions," he said.

"Young man, was there something in the demeanor of this private detective, Donald Lam, which caused you to believe he had seen something?"

"Yes."

"What was it?"

"Well, he was walking along, walking along, walking along, and I was watching him, and all of a sudden he stopped still and then turned and started walking out into the alfalfa field; and then he stood with his back to me so I couldn't see what he was doing and then all of a sudden he turned and started back toward the bank of the ditch."

"And what did you do?"

"As soon as I saw that he had found something, I ran across the muddy bottom of the ditch, up the bank on the other side, and over in the alfalfa field to where he was standing."

"Did you run very fast?"

165

"Very fast indeed, sir. I have my feet very tough. I can run over rocks and the roughness in the ground just as though I had shoes on—better than if I have shoes on."

"So then what happened?" the judge asked.

"When this man saw that I knew he had found something was when he told me to go to my parents and have them call the police."

"Now that, if the Court please," Newberry said, "is purely a conclusion of the witness, incompetent, irrelevant and immaterial, calling for—"

"Just a minute," Judge Polk said. "The objection will be temporarily sustained, but I want to ask this young man a few more questions.

"Just what did Mr. Lam do which was out of the ordinary?"

"Well, he started walking toward the bank of the ditch. Then he had taken a couple of steps and saw me coming, running just as fast as I could to join him."

"So what did you do?"

"I asked him, 'What did you find, mister,' and he didn't answer me right away. He sort of thought things over for a little while and then he said, 'Never mind, but go home at once—do you live near here?'

"I told him I did.

"He said, 'Go home and tell your father to call the police and have them come out at once.'

"So then I said, 'What did you find?' and he didn't say anything, so then I did a little looking and I saw this gun."

"Was it in plain sight from where you were standing?"

"Not in plain sight, but I would have seen it even if he hadn't said anything. It was lying where the sun was glinting on the metal enough so that you could see there was something in the alfalfa."

"I think that tells the story in a manner which is admissible in evidence," Judge Polk said. "Do counsel for either side wish to ask any more questions?"

"This covers the evidence that I expected this young man to give," Roberts said.

"Is there any cross-examination?" Judge Polk asked Newberry.

"Newberry shook his head emphatically. "No questions," he said. "I do move, however, to strike out all of the evidence of this witness on the ground that he is too young to understand the meaning of the oath."

"Motion denied."

"Upon the further ground that the testimony given by this witness is purely speculative, is not objective, and relates to conclusions formed by this witness."

"The motion is denied," Judge Polk said. "I will admit that some of the testimony given by this witness relates to conclusions which he formed in his own mind. But in each instance the basis of those conclusions is set forth objectively in the form of admissible evidence so that any interpolation of what the witness thought or conclusions he reached from what he had seen are immaterial. This is an interesting bit of evidence and I don't mind stating that the Court is impressed by it, although, of course, at the present time I don't understand just what it is leading up to.

"Is it your contention, Mr. Prosecutor, that this murder weapon was in the possession of Donald Lam, that it was taken out into the field by Donald Lam and surreptitiously dropped at the spot where it was found?"

"That is correct, Your Honor," Roberts said.

"Very well, go ahead with the case," Judge Polk observed, glancing thoughtfully at me.

Roberts called a man by the name of Smith who testified that he was a semi-pro ball player; that he played the position of pitcher; that he had been taken to the scene of the crime by Sergeant Sellers; that he had been given a revolver which was an exact duplicate of the gun introduced as People's Exhibit B; that it was a Smith & Wesson chambered for five shells with a one-and-seven-eighths-inch barrel; that he had stood by the ditch at the scene of the crime and had thrown the gun as far as he could; that he had thrown it not once but several times, and that he had never been able to throw the gun as far as the spot in which the gun had been found when the police officers arrived.

"Any questions on cross-examination?" Roberts asked.

Newberry shook his head.

"Just a minute, Your Honor," I said. "Since my integrity is being impugned here, I would like to ask one question, whether or not the man tried throwing the gun from a point farther down the bank or whether he stood right at the scene of the crime. There is no evidence that the person who threw the gun had to stand at the exact scene of the crime and—"

"Now, just a minute," Judge Polk said. "You are out of order, Mr. Lam, although I appreciate the point you are making. If counsel for the defense wishes to bring out that point, he certainly is entitled to do so. On the other hand, as far as this Court is concerned, it is a self-evident fact. The diagram now shows the alfalfa field and the spot where the gun was picked up. Quite apparently, by moving down the bank of the ditch, and throwing the gun straight across, instead of at a diagonal, quite a few feet could have been saved. That is a matter of simple mathematics."

"Just a moment, Your Honor," Roberts said. "It stands to reason that if the murderer threw that gun he wanted to get rid of it just as soon as possible. He would have left the trailer, run to the bank of the ditch, trying to dispose of the gun, seen the muddy bottom in the ditch, and so decided to throw the gun as far as he could."

"Are you," Judge Polk asked, "trying to argue with the Court?"

Roberts thought for a moment, then said, "Well, yes, Your Honor."

"Don't do it," Judge Polk said. "There is no more reason for the murderer to have run directly from the scene of the crime at a right angle than there is for him to have angled down so that he came to the bank of the ditch at a point that was right opposite from the place where the gun was found."

Roberts hesitated for a moment, then sat down.

"Call your next witness," Judge Polk said.

Roberts said, "I call Maybelle Dillon to the stand."

Maybelle Dillon was in her late forties, with a flat chest, sagging shoulders, and a general air of despondency, but her eyes were alert and she spoke with a rapid-fire delivery.

She gave her address as 895 Billinger Street, Los Angeles, and her occupation as a typist.

"For whom do you type?" Roberts asked.

"I am a free-lance typist. I type manuscripts and do minor editing. I advertise in the writer's magazines and get quite a number of manuscripts in the mail. I give these minor editing, type them in acceptable form, and send them back, together with one copy at so much per page."

"Are you acquainted with one Nanncie Beaver?"

"Oh, yes, yes indeed!"

"And where does Miss Beaver live?

"At Eight-thirty Billinger Street, Apartment Sixty-two B."

"Have you had occasion to see Miss Beaver in the last week?"

"Yes, sir."

"When?"

"It was—now, let me see, it was the fifteenth of the month."

"And where were you at that time?"

"I was in Nanncie's apartment."

"Do you do work for Nanncie?"

"No, sir, she does her own typing, but we're very good friends, and Nanncie occasionally comes up with a client for me, some beginning author who either doesn't have a typewriter or who can't think on a typewriter or who doesn't turn out good enough work for submission to the magazines . . . you see I work with amateurs."

"Was anybody else present at that time when you saw Miss Beaver?"

"No, sir, there were just the two of us."

"Now, at that time, did Nanncie show you a gun?"

"Yes, sir."

"I show you a gun, People's Exhibit B, and ask you if that looks like the gun that she showed you at that time."

The witness handled the gun gingerly and said, "Yes, sir, it looks very much like the gun."

"And what did Nanncie tell you?"

"She told me that she had tipped off one of her writer friends to a dope-smuggling racket and that he was about to write it up; that one of her friends, a Mr. Calhoun—"

"Just a minute, just a minute," Newberry interrupted, on his feet, his voice filling the courtroom. "This is improper and counsel knows it. This is irrelevant, immaterial, and is hearsay. It is completely outside of the issues. Unless it can be shown that the defendant was there or unless the witness heard the words of the defendant, anything that this Nanncie Beaver told her about the source of the gun is completely irrelevant."

"I think that's right," Judge Polk said.

"May I be heard?" Roberts asked.

"You may be heard, but this conversation seems to me to be hearsay."

"Surely, Your Honor," Roberts said, "we have here a murder weapon. We have this weapon in the hands of the very close friend of the defendant. We have—"

"Object to that statement as prejudicial misconduct. I move it be stricken from the record," Newberry shouted.

"It will go out," Judge Polk ruled. "Now, try to confine yourself, Mr. Prosecutor, to the facts of this case as they are admissible in court."

"We expect to prove a friendship, Your Honor. We expect to prove that statements as to this gun are really part of the *res gestae*."

Judge Polk shook his head. "You can't do it by hearsay."

"Very well," Roberts said, "we'll go at it another way. I'll excuse this witness from the stand and I'll call Mrs. George Honcutt to the stand, please."

Mrs. Honcutt was a matronly woman with square shoulders, big hips and a bulldog jaw. She came swinging up to the witness stand like a full-rigged ship plowing into the harbor.

"What is your name, address and occupation?" the clerk asked.

"Mrs. George Honcutt. I manage the Maple Leaf Motel in Calexico."

"I ask you if, on the early morning of the twentieth of this month, you had a tenant in your motel by the name of Nanncie Beaver?"

"I did."

"How was she registered?"

"Under the name of Nanncie Beaver, but she first tried to register under the name of Nanncie Armstrong."

"And what caused her to change her registration?"

"I said, 'Look, dearie, when a single woman comes in here I have to know something about her. Now, I want to take a look at your driving license.' So then she produced her driving license and said she was sort of hiding and didn't want anyone to know she was registered there, and I told her it was all right by me as long as she behaved herself; that I was running a decent, respectable place and that I'd expect her to behave herself, otherwise out she went."

"And she stayed on there?"

"Yes."

"Until what time?"

"I don't know when she actually left the motel, but the rent was paid up until the twentieth. When I went in to check her room on the morning of the twentieth, there was the key in the door on the outside and she had gone. All of her baggage—everything."

"Was the rent paid?"

"You bet the rent was paid," Mrs. Honcutt said. "With a woman like that I collect in advance, day by day."

"Thank you, that's all," Roberts said.

"Any questions?" Judge Polk asked Newberry.

The lawyer seemed puzzled. "No questions."

"Now then," Roberts said, "I'm going to call Mr. Herbert C. Newton."

Herbert Newton was a middle-aged individual with a quick, nervous manner and a wiry frame. He quite evidently enjoyed being a witness.

He gave his name, address and occupation to the clerk, then turned expectantly to Roberts.

Roberts said, "Where were you staying on the evening of the nineteenth and the morning of the twentieth?"

"At the Maple Leaf Motel in Calexico."

"At any time during the night did you have occasion to get up and look out of your window?"

"I did."

"What was your unit?"

"I was in Unit One which is right next to the street and right across from Unit Twelve."

"And what happened, if anything?"

"It was around two or three o'clock in the morning when I heard voices across in Unit Twelve, and the light came on in Unit Twelve which threw a light in my bedroom. The voices and the light wakened me and kept me from sleeping. I became very irritated."

"And what did you do?"

"After a while I got up."

"And what did you see or hear?"

"I could hear a man's voice and a woman's voice. They seemed to be arguing. After I got up out of bed I heard the man say, 'You've got to get out of here. You're in danger. You come with me and I'll take you to another place where you won't get mixed up with this writer friend and be in danger.'"

"Anything else?"

"Yes. He said, 'Get packed and meet me out in the car and I'll take the gun. You can't keep it with you in Mexico.'"

"What was that last?"

"He said, 'I'll take the gun.'"

"And then what happened?"

"Then he said, 'Pack just as fast as you can.'"

"Anything else?"

"Yes. He said. 'You're foolish to have got mixed in this thing. Now, I'll take charge of things and get you off the hook, but you've got to quit being tied up with that crazy writer.'"

"Then what happened?"

"Then the door opened and this man came out."

"Did you get a good look at him?"

"I certainly did. The light from inside the apartment was full on his face."

"And do you see this man in the courtroom?"

"Certainly. He is the defendant."

"That's the man you saw emerging from the apartment?"

"That's the man I saw."

"That's the man who said, 'I'll take the gun'?"

"That's the man who said, 'I'll take the gun. You can't keep it with you in Mexico.'"

"Then what happened?"

"Then the door was closed, and after a very few minutes the light went out and some woman whom I couldn't see opened the door and put a bag and a suitcase on the threshold, and this man who had been waiting in a big car, parked at the curb, came and picked up the bag and the suitcase and put them in the car. Then they drove away."

"Any questions on cross-examination?" Judge Polk asked.

Newberry said, "I have just one or two questions of this witness.

"Can you give us the exact time of this conversation, Mr. Newton?"

"No, I cannot. I was aroused from sleep and I was annoyed and irritated. In fact, I was so angry I couldn't get back to sleep for I guess an hour. I know it was before three o'clock because I didn't get to sleep until after three o'clock. I finally got up and took a couple of Bufferin."

"There's no question in your mind that the man you saw was Milton Carling Calhoun, the defendant in this case?"

"Absolutely no question."

"Do you wear glasses?"

"I wear glasses when I read, but I can see without glasses at a distance and I saw this man just as plain as day, standing there in the doorway."

"I think that's all," Newberry said.

Roberts said, "If the Court please, that concludes our case. We ask that the defendant be bound over to the Superior Court on a charge of first-degree murder."

I said to Newberry, "Ask for a continuance."

Newberry shook his head. "It won't do any good. We aren't

going to put on any defense. I never put on a defense at a pre-liminary hearing. It just tips your hand and—"

I interrupted him to say in a whisper, "They haven't proven anything except a bare case of circumstantial evidence and—"

"Don't be funny," Newberry broke in. "They've shown his fingerprints on the houseboat. They've shown his owner-ship of the fatal gun. They have evidence showing that he went to the Maple Leaf Motel at two o'clock in the morn-ing to get the gun. He was going to take care of things to pro-tect his light-of-love. He went out and took matters into his own hands. He killed the dope runner."

"That's not the kind of a man Calhoun is," I said. "For God's sake, move for a continuance!"

Judge Polk said, "Gentlemen, is there any defense?"

"A half hour's continuance," I said.

Calhoun looked at me and then looked at his attorney.

"A half-hour continuance won't hurt anything," he said to Newberry.

Newberry got to his feet reluctantly.

"There seems to be some question as to procedure," he said. "May I ask for a thirty-minute recess?"

Judge Polk looked at his watch. "The Court will take a fifteen-minute recess," he said. "That should be ample for counsel to confer with his client."

Judge Polk left the bench and retired to chambers.

I grabbed Newberry's arm and pulled him and Calhoun over to a secluded corner of the courtroom under the watch-ful eye of the deputy sheriff who had Calhoun in custody.

"You lied to me," Newberry said to his client.

Calhoun said, "I only lied to you on an unessential matter. It was absolutely vital to me to keep Nanncie out of it. Yes, I did go to the motel. I wanted to get the gun back be-cause I had an idea that I was going to stay and protect

Nanncie. But she told me she didn't have the gun, that she had given it to this writer, this Colburn Hale."

"And that made you mad?" I asked.

"It made me *very* angry. I had given her that gun for her own protection."

"So what did you do?"

"I took her over to the Lucerna Hotel in Mexicali, got her a room and paid for it. Then I came back across the border and registered at the De Anza Hotel."

I shook my head and said, "No, you didn't. You drove along the road to that place where the pickup was parked. Now, what caused you to go in that houseboat?"

"I didn't go in the houseboat," Calhoun said.

"All right, what did happen?"

Calhoun said dejectedly, "I have held out on you people. I shouldn't have done it, but I was trying to protect myself."

"Go on, go on," I said. "We haven't got all day. What happened?"

Calhoun said, "When I was driving into Calexico my headlights picked up this pickup and the houseboat on the trailer, and as they did I saw a man jump out of the door of the houseboat, hit the ground in a flying leap and start running just as fast as he could go over toward that drainage ditch. After he got a few yards over there on an angle, he got out of the range of my headlights."

"And what did you do?"

"It was around two o'clock in the morning. I stopped my car, went over to the houseboat and called out, 'Is everything all right?'

"There was no answer. I rapped with my knuckles on the door. There was no answer. I started to try the door. That was probably when I put my left hand against the side of the houseboat to brace myself. And then I thought better of it. After all, it wasn't any of my business. I called out again, 'Is everything all right in there?' I received no answer so I got back in my car and drove on to Calexico.

"I went at once to the Maple Leaf Motel and I did have the conversation with Nanncie that this man overheard. I took Nanncie across the border to a hotel where I thought she would be safer than in that Maple Leaf Motel. And I wanted to get her out of the clutches of that writer friend of hers."

"What about the gun?"

"I did tell her that I'd take the gun back because I knew it would make complications if she had a gun across the border in Mexico, and she told me she didn't have it, that she'd loaned it to Hale.

"I'll admit I became angry. I had given her that gun for her personal protection. Certainly not with the idea that she was going to pass it around to some down-at-the-heel writer friend."

I turned to Newberry. "All right," I said, "you're going to have to use heroic measures."

"What do you mean?"

I said, "They're going to bind him over for trial unless you pull a fast one."

"They're going to bind him over for trial in any event. I'm not even going to object. I'm not going to put up a whisper of an argument except that I'm going to put up the old song and dance that there's nothing in this case except circumstantial evidence; that they can show that the murder was committed with his gun and that there are fingerprints on the houseboat, but they can't tell when those fingerprints were made or who was holding the gun when it was fired. The fingerprints may have been made at any time."

"And your client is going to get bound over."

"He'll get bound over."

I looked at Calhoun. "Do you like that?"

"Good God, no!" Calhoun said.

"But you can't stop it," Newberry said. "He's stuck."

"Not if you play it right," I told him.

Newberry looked at me with sudden distaste. "Are you," he asked, "now trying to tell me how I should handle this case?"

I looked right back at him and said, "Yes."

"Well, don't do it," Newberry warned. "I don't know just how you fit into the picture, Lam, but I think you're in this thing up to your necktie. Are you sure that you weren't the man Calhoun saw running out of the houseboat trailer?"

"I'm sure I wasn't the man he saw," I said, "and if you use your head a little bit we may be able to knock this whole thing into a cocked hat right now."

"You're crazy," he told me. "It's an axiom of criminal law that you can't do anything on a preliminary examination. You cross-examine the witnesses, you get as much of the prosecution's case as you can, and then you just ride along with the punch."

"To hell with the axioms of criminal law," I said. "I'm talking about a particular case. This case. You let Calhoun be bound over and there will be headlines all over the country."

"We can't control the press," Newberry said. "We have a free press in this country. They can print the news any way they want to just so they confine themselves to the truth.

"Now then, a feminine angle has been introduced into this case and, believe me, that's going to give the newspapers a field day. MILLIONAIRE DEFENDANT IN SURREPTITIOUS MIDNIGHT RENDEZVOUS . . ."

I said to Calhoun, "Do you want to put on a defense?"

"I want to get out of this," he said.

"It isn't what Calhoun wants, it's what *I* want," Newberry said. "I'm the lawyer and I don't brook any interference from

a client. I'll tell you right now, Lam, I don't brook any interference from some smart-aleck private detective either."

"I'm not a smart-aleck private detective," I told him. "I'm
a damn good detective."

Calhoun looked from one to the other.

"What do you want to do, Calhoun?" I asked. "Make up
your mind."

"I guess there's nothing I can do," Calhoun said. "Newberry has reached a decision."

"And who is Newberry working for?"

"Why . . . I guess he's working . . . he's working for
me."

"I don't work for anybody," Newberry said. "I'm a professional man. I'm an attorney. I permit myself to be retained
in cases. I go to court and I handle those cases my way. Make
no mistake about it, *my way.*"

Calhoun shrugged his shoulders and looked helplessly at
me.

I said, "You want my judgment, Calhoun? I think we can
spring you out of this. In fact, I'm pretty damn sure we can."

"I'll bet a thousand to one against it," Newberry said.

"I'll take a hundred dollars of that right now," I told him.

He said angrily, "I don't want to make any actual bet. I
was just simply giving the odds. It wouldn't do any good to
make an actual bet because I'm going to stand up and tell
the Court that we consent to an order binding the defendant
over."

I looked at Calhoun and said, "Fire him!"

"What?" Calhoun asked incredulously.

"Fire him!" I said.

Newberry looked at me and said, "Why, you smart-aleck
son of a . . ."

I turned away from him and said to Calhoun, "He's your

lawyer. You fire him and do as I say and you'll get out of this."

"So you're practicing law," Newberry said.

"I'm telling Calhoun what to do. Calhoun can be his own attorney. You do what I tell you to, Calhoun, and we'll be home free."

Calhoun looked dubious.

The door from chambers opened and Judge Polk came in. The bailiff rapped the Court to order. We all stood up, then were seated.

"Very well," Judge Polk said, "we will take up the case of People versus Calhoun. Is there any defense?"

"Fire him," I said to Calhoun. "Now!"

Calhoun reached a sudden decision. He got to his feet and said, "Your Honor, I want to be my own lawyer."

Judge Polk was startled. Roberts whirled around and looked at us as though we had all taken leave of our senses.

"You want to discharge your lawyer?" Judge Polk asked.

Newberry grabbed up his briefcase. "There's no need to discharge *me*," he said. "I'm quitting the case."

"Now, just a moment," Judge Polk said. "You can't quit the case without the consent of the Court."

Newberry hesitated and said, "I don't want any more of this client. I don't want any part of him or of this smart-aleck private detective."

"Just control yourself," Judge Polk said. "Mr. Calhoun, what seems to be the situation?"

"I want to put on a defense and I want to conduct my own case," Calhoun said.

"You want to discharge your lawyer?"

"I want to discharge him."

Judge Polk looked at Newberry. "You want to withdraw from the case?"

"I withdraw from the case. I have withdrawn. I do withdraw. I don't want any more to do with it."

Judge Polk sighed. "Very well," he said, "the order will be granted. The defendant will act for himself in *propria persona*.

"Now then, Mr. Calhoun, do you wish to put on any witness?"

"Call Colburn Hale," I whispered.

Calhoun looked at me, then looked at the indignant back of Newberry who was stalking out of the courtroom.

"I'll call Colburn Hale as my first witness," he said.

While Colburn Hale came limping forward and held up his right hand as though his entire body hurt, Calhoun whispered, "What the devil do I ask him?"

"Sit down beside me," I said, "and ask the questions as I feed them to you."

I whispered to Calhoun, while Hale was giving his name, address and occupation to the clerk, "Make your questions as short as possible and encourage him to do the talking.

"Now, your first question is whether or not he ever saw the gun, People's Exhibit B. Hand the gun to him and ask him if he ever saw it, and if he says, 'Yes,' ask him when was the last time he saw it. Encourage the guy to talk."

Calhoun was as awkward as a man trying to water-ski for the first time. He floundered around and said to the clerk, "Please show this witness the gun and I want to ask him if he ever saw that gun before."

"What is the object of this?" Judge Polk asked.

Calhoun looked at me.

I said, "We want to find out how the gun got into that field."

Calhoun passed my comment on to the judge.

"Very well," Judge Polk said. "I think that is probably a legitimate part of the defense, since the prosecution has made a point of it. Let the witness answer the question."

"I have seen the gun before," Hale said.

"Where? How? When? And what happened to it? When did it leave his possession?" I asked Calhoun.

"When did you see it?"

"I saw it—well, I guess it was about the seventeenth."

"How did you get it?"

"Nanncie Beaver gave it to me. She told me that—"

"Just a minute," Roberts said. "We object to any conversation between the witness and Nanncie Beaver."

"Sustained," Judge Polk said.

"When did you last have the gun?" Calhoun asked.

"I lost it on the evening of the nineteenth."

"How did you lose it?"

"Puggy took it from me."

Calhoun looked at me.

"Who's Puggy?" I whispered to him.

"Who's Puggy?" he asked. "Tell me all about it."

Hale said, "I was on the track of this dope shipment. I had this gun. I was following the dope shipment up from San Felipe. I thought I was being smart.

"I didn't know there was a tail car behind me. When we got almost to where the La Puerta road turns off, this tail car closed in on me and crowded me to the side of the road. Then the pickup with the houseboat trailer stopped.

"The man who was driving the tail car was evidently a pugilist, because the other guy called him Puggy. He started working me over. I tried to pull the gun on him and the man from the dope car—I guess that was Eddie Sutton—had me covered and said, 'Get your hands up, or your brains will get smattered all over the side of your car.'"

I nudged Calhoun. "Tell him to go on."

"Go on," Calhoun said.

I whispered to Calhoun, "Every time he stops talking, just tell him, 'Go on.'"

Calhoun nodded.

"Well," Hale said, "they really worked me over. That's where I got this shiner, and I got a bloody nose and a cut lip. There was blood all over my shirt and I was pretty much of a mess by the time they got done with me."

"Go on," Calhoun said.

"They got me down and they kicked me and really gave me a beating. Then they put me in my car, tied me up with some kind of a thin, strong cord, sort of like a fishing line—that is, a heavy fishing line—and they drove me down the side road, put a gag in my mouth, parked the car and said, 'Now, stay there, you smart son of a bitch. That'll teach you to interfere in things that don't concern you.'"

"Go on," Calhoun said.

"They took the gun. The man called Puggy took the gun."

"Go on," Calhoun said.

"Well, that's all of it," Hale went on, "except the fact that about—I don't know—seven o'clock in the morning—eight o'clock, I guess, this very fine Mexican gentleman by the name of José Chapalla came along and saw my car by the side of the road. He stopped to take a look and saw me tied and gagged and he untied the ropes and took the gag out of my mouth. I was about half dead by that time, and José Chapalla took me to his home and they gave me coffee and some eggs and tortillas and then I went to sleep, and then José took me back to my car and after a long while I drove away. I started for Mexicali and got as far as a roadside restaurant where I went in to get some beer, and that's where Donald Lam and Nanncie Beaver found me."

"Ask him if he's sore and stiff," I said.

"Are you sore and stiff?" Calhoun asked.

"Of course I am! My ribs are just about caved in. I'm more sore now than I was the day of the beating. I not only have this black eye, but I'm afraid my ribs are cracked."

"Tell him to show us the bruises," I whispered to Calhoun.

"Can you show us the bruises?" Calhoun asked.

Hale pointed to his eye.

"On his ribs, on his sides, on his torso," I said.

"The other bruises," Calhoun said. "Where are they?"

Hale put a hand tenderly to his side. "All over."

"Show us," I said.

"Show us," Calhoun echoed.

"What do you mean, show you?" Hale demanded.

"Pull up your shirt," I whispered.

"Pull up your shirt," Calhoun echoed.

Hale looked at us and suddenly there was panic in his eyes. "I'm not going to disrobe here in public," he said.

"Just show us a bruise," I whispered. "Show us a bruise on your arm. Show us a bruise anywhere on your torso—just one single bruise—one black-and-blue mark."

Calhoun stammered, "Show us your body, show us anything that's black and blue."

"I don't have to," Hale said.

Calhoun seemed to be at an impasse.

"Tell him he's a liar," I said. "Tell him he can't show us a single bruise, that he hasn't got a spot on his body. Ask that the Court appoint a doctor to examine him."

Calhoun ran his fingers through his hair and said, "How about having a doctor make an examination, Your Honor? This man hasn't got a bruise on his body."

"He'd have to have," Judge Polk said.

"He's lying," Calhoun said.

"Wait a minute," Roberts said. "You can't impeach your own witness. I don't like to be technical with a man who is putting on his own defense, but we have to protect the rights of the people. He can't impeach his own witness."

I said, "Ask the judge if he wants to get at the truth in the case."

Calhoun was good that time. He said, "Does Your Honor want to get at the truth of this case or not?"

Judge Polk looked at the uncomfortable Colburn Hale and hesitated.

"Just a minute," Roberts said. "Who's trying this case? What does this private detective think he's trying to do? Donald Lam isn't an attorney. He doesn't appear in the case. He has no standing in court."

It was too much for Hale. He jumped out of the witness chair and scurried like a rabbit for the side door of the courtroom.

"Stop that man!" Judge Polk yelled at the bailiff.

They couldn't stop him. Hale was long gone.

I looked at the judge and said, "He recovered from all that stiffness and soreness pretty fast, didn't he, Your Honor?"

Judge Polk looked down at me, started to rebuke me, then suddenly smiled and said, "He did for a fact.

"I would suggest that the Sheriff's Office put out an all-points bulletin for this man. His black eye should make it very easy to pick him up."

"But this Donald Lam doesn't have any right to ask questions in this case," Roberts objected.

Polk smiled at him and said, "Quite right, Mr. Roberts, but this Court *does* have the right to ask questions and this Court intends to ask some very searching questions."

The officers caught Hale at the courthouse door and returned him to court.

Judge Polk said, "Young man, you are on the witness stand. Now, you get right back there in that witness chair and you listen to me.

"It appears that you may have committed a crime. The Court warns you that you don't have to make any statement whatever. If you feel it may incriminate you, you don't have to talk. Or, if you just want to keep quiet, you have that privilege. You are entitled to have an attorney represent you at all stages of the proceeding and if you don't have money enough to get an attorney, the Court will appoint one. But you aren't going to get up off that witness stand and run out of the courtroom the way you did a moment ago.

"Now then, do you care to answer questions?"

Hale shifted his position and said nothing.

"Do you want an attorney to advise you? The Court is going to call a doctor to examine you."

Hale said, "I may as well come clean. I haven't got any way out, and, after all, I acted in self-defense. If I keep on being as foolish as I have been, I'll wind up facing a murder rap."

"You can either talk or not talk, just as you want," Judge Polk said, "but you're going to be examined."

Hale started talking, the words just pouring out of his mouth. He said, "I knew that dope shipment was coming across the border. I knew that they intended to make a rendezvous with the driver of a scout car at the Monte Carlo Café at seven o'clock. I told my girl friend that I would meet her there at seven o'clock.

"It started to rain. The shipment was delayed. I followed it across the border. There were two men in the car. One of the men picked up the scout car and went on ahead. The pickup with the houseboat trailer parked by the side of the road.

"I had the story I wanted. It was one whale of a story, but I didn't have it all. I wanted to see where they took this houseboat. I sensed the scout car had found a roadblock or something that caused a delay.

"I stayed where I could keep the houseboat under surveillance. It was a rainy night. I waited and waited. The driver of the pickup had gone back into the houseboat. I had an idea he'd gone to sleep.

"I was overly confident. I was a plain fool. I couldn't resist trying to get one detail I hadn't been able to get and that was the license number of the pickup. Because of the houseboat that number was hard to see. I felt the man who was driving the pickup had gone to sleep in the houseboat. I sneaked up, hoping I could get the number I wanted—and I walked right into a trap. This man had spotted me and he suddenly opened the door, held a gun on me and ordered me to get into the houseboat.

"I knew it was either him or me. He wasn't sure just what I was doing there. I could tell from the way he acted he didn't think I was an officer. He wanted to know what I wanted and what I was doing snooping around. Well, he got just a little careless. I suddenly jerked out my gun and said, 'Stick 'em up.' I was nervous. I waited maybe a tenth of a second to see what he was going to do. I waited too long. He fired. If the officers will look in that houseboat, they'll find a bullet hole somewhere near the front of the boat.

"I fired at about the same time he did. He missed. I didn't.

"I got in a panic. I took his gun, put it in my pocket and threw it away a couple of hours later. I took the Calhoun gun and ran down toward the place where I had parked my car and then threw the gun across the ditch as far as I could throw it.

"Then, instead of going to the police the way I should have done, I drove down across the border and tried to think of some way out of the mess. I stayed in the car all night. Finally, when one of the stores opened up, I bought some fishline and tied myself up at a place where I felt certain I'd be discovered. If I went too long without being discovered

I could untie myself, but I felt certain I could get away with my story.

"I hit myself a good punch in the eye, bloodied my nose, and I made up that story about having been beaten up and kicked. It hadn't occurred to me that people would be looking for black-and-blue marks on my body.

"Donald Lam kept trying to get me in the swimming pool at the hotel, and that was when I realized how vulnerable I was. My story wouldn't stand up if— Well, I don't want to get blamed for murder. I acted in self-defense."

Judge Polk looked down at Sergeant Sellers. "Did the officers," he asked, "make a careful examination of the front of that houseboat to see if there was a bullet hole in the boat?"

"There was no hole in the boat, Your Honor," Sellers said, "but there was a sofa pillow on the davenport that had a very small hole in it. We didn't take the pillow to pieces to see if there was a bullet on the inside of it."

"You'd better do that," Judge Polk said, and then added gratuitously, "It seems to me that the police work in this case has been slightly below par.

"The sheriff will take this man into custody. The case against Milton Carling Calhoun is dismissed.

"Court's adjourned."

Judge Polk left the bench and there was pandemonium in the courtroom. A couple of newspaper reporters got jammed in the door as they ran simultaneously for the nearest telephone.

I looked over at Calhoun and said, "Congratulations!"

The guy grabbed me in an embrace. I was afraid he might try to kiss me.

It took us nearly half an hour to get past the newspaper reporters and out to my car. I managed to get Calhoun to say "No comment" often enough to make the newspapermen give up, but the television men kept hounding us with portable cameras.

Finally we got free.

I gave Calhoun a road map. "What's this?" he asked.

"A map of the road to El Golfo."

"What's at El Golfo?"

"Nanncie Beaver," I said.

"Why at El Golfo?"

"That's so you can go down and get her without any newspaper reporters tailing you—that is, if you're smart. Then you can come into our office the first of next week and settle up."

He looked at me with dawning comprehension, then he gripped my hand, hard.

16

Bertha Cool was in rare form. She teetered back and forth in her squeaky swivel chair; her eyes were as hard as the diamonds on her hands.

"Now, you listen to me, Mr. Milton Carling Calhoun," she said. "You're supposed to be a big businessman. You're supposed to know your way around.

"What the hell was the idea of coming in here and getting us to go on a wild-goose chase, looking for Colburn Hale when what you really wanted was to find his girl friend?"

Calhoun squirmed uneasily.

"I had heard that private detective agencies sometimes blackmailed their clients," he said. "So I tried to conceal my background. I simply couldn't afford to have my name associated with that of Nanncie Beaver. If I had told you what I really wanted . . . Well, I would have left myself wide open."

"So," Bertha Cool said, "you led with your chin. And what makes me sore is the fact that you came in here trying to put us on the defensive, pretending that you didn't know anything about the agency, pretending that Donald was too slight to do the work, and that I wasn't any good because I was a woman.

"Get out your checkbook, Mr. Milton Calhoun. I'm going to hit you between the eyes."

"You agreed to a certain per diem," Calhoun said weakly. "I will boost that, of course, but after all . . ."

Bertha came forward in her chair with a thump, leaned her elbows on the desk, glittered at Calhoun. "And what happened?" she said. "You lied to us. You threw us off on a false track. You put Donald in terrific danger. You . . ."

"I know, I know. I'm sorry," Calhoun said. "I'm prepared to pay something extra."

"How much?" Bertha Cool asked.

"Bearing in mind that Donald Lam gave me the best legal advice I ever had," Calhoun said, "I had intended to add a gratuity to the amount of the bill."

"How much?"

Calhoun took a deep breath. "I want your complete silence," he said. "No word of what I wanted must ever come out of this. I must have complete secrecy."

"How much?" Bertha Cool asked.

Calhoun reached in his pocket and pulled out a checkbook. "I have made out a check for ten thousand dollars," he said, "which I hope will cover the per diem expenses and the gratuity."

Bertha's jaw sagged open for a minute. She blinked her eyes a couple of times.

"Fry me for an oyster," she said.

And then there was a flash of light as her jeweled hand reached for the check.

"And, for your confidential information," Calhoun went on, "I am completely changing my life. I am sick and tired of the artificial existence I have been living, thinking only of money, money, money.

"From now on I am going to try to develop my creative energy. In short, I am going to take up writing, and I have a new address. It is Eight-seventeen Billinger Street. I am moving into the apartment vacated by Colburn Hale."

And the guy positively beamed at us.

Bertha Cool folded the check and said, "Fry me for an oyster—no, damn it, poach me for an egg!"

Calhoun grinned. "Without breaking the yolk—sunny side up," he said.

I reached across and shook the guy's hand.